To Dance with Death Beneath the Falling Stars

A very short novel

STEPHEN R WAGNER

ISBN: 1502472708
ISBN-13: 978-1502472700

This book has no chapters.*

It begins and just is. If you lose your place in it, you will eventually find a way back - (and if you don't, you weren't meant to).

*I was tempted at one point to have chapters. I even considered having chapters with exotic names. I was speaking once with The Conversationalist, on the phone, and we talked about the violence in the book and of what style it was. I said something to the effect that it was very violent but at least the villain wasn't torturing kittens. We both, of course, instantly realized that this was something which might need to happen. We spent several minutes coming up with chapter titles that alluded to this in varying ways: arriving at names such as "Kitty Trouble" and "Pussy Peril" but in the end, we decided that it would probably not be appropriate to include such things in the book. (Besides, I would then have to come up with dozens of other chapter titles as well.) So I left them out.**

It is, of course, going to need chapters after all. As it (the story) has quick changes of direction and perspective that need to be delineated. I didn't want it to have chapters, but it needs them. What can I do? Take them away? I don't think so.*

***But I'm not going to name them.

CONTENTS

The Table of Contents

We all do what we can
So we can do just one more thing
We can all be free
Maybe not with words
Maybe not with a look
But with your mind

-Cat Power (Maybe Not)

Stephen R Wagner

ONE

I was a beat cop on the south side of Chicago fighting ennui and childhood obesity, when a malignant gang caught me at the edge of the highway and messed up my colon. This is the story of how I battled that gang and then chased down their leader, Cancertalkerous Melonomames.

Melonomames was a tough bastard, who was trained in guerrilla warfare in the foothills of southern New Hampshire. He was a known killer who went for everything: women, children, small woodland creatures, the elderly. He loved to kill the elderly. Nothing was beyond him. He killed with immunity and impunity. Sometimes he killed quickly. But sometimes he didn't. Sometimes he dragged it out over enormous stretches of time, torturing unimaginably as he went.

Everyone was afraid of him, including myself. What he

didn't know, though, was that his men had botched their initial hit on me. They hadn't wholeheartedly been after me, but had only gone after me on a momentary whim, which was their tremendous mistake, for which I was grateful. His foot soldiers had been inefficient, and for now, at least, I was still alive. I knew who was responsible because the traffic cameras had caught his men on film. Melonomames's gang all wore the same black jackets with red arm bands that had disorganized crushed ovals stacked up on each other in what appeared to be random order. But they had randomly messed with the wrong man, and I was going to go after them - faster and harder than determinism.

I had been out on an adventure on my motorcycle when they got to me.

The gang members had been coming out of a coffee shop on the edge of town. They were laughing and carrying bags to their cars. A woman from the coffee shop ran out, shouted something at them, and one of the gang members started back to deal with her - when I pulled into the parking lot between the woman and the gang.

They all stopped.

Their leader whistled, pointed to me, and then circled the air with his finger. It was Lymphatico, Cancertalkerous Melonomames's first lieutenant. All the henchmen ran to their cars and motorcycles. I leaned over and turned off the auxiliary electric handlebar warmer, on the dash of my motorcycle, as I was going to need all the juice the small motorcycle had.

I signaled with my hand, for the woman to stay where she was, and then popped a wheelie by throwing the bike into second gear and gassing it.

I took off, across the intersection, towards the on-ramp that led onto the interstate, with the gang in close pursuit behind me.

TWO

[I should, perhaps, tell you at this point that I have never been a beat cop, and I have only ever travelled past south Chicago on the highway, when I visited that part of the country many years ago. In fact, I live in a semi-rural town near the northern tip of Massachusetts. I am not an officer of the law, but I choose to help uphold universal law, privately, and I am supported by a surprisingly large network of contacts both in and out of a large variety of organizations. I have earned their trust and they have earned mine - as there is too much out there that must be battled, for them to go it all alone. And, although some would perhaps say I shouldn't, I have the awesome power of fiction behind me. And, my dear friends, if you do it right, and you do it well, there is nothing you can't do in fiction. It is a lever, a giant pry-bar, wedged between the earth and the thick darkness of space, and we are pushing on that pry-bar now. Pushing it forward. Leveraging the world, and everything in it.]

~

As I brought the bike up to full speed and began to merge onto the interstate, three cars of gang members (followed by others on motorcycles) pulled up in a line close behind me. I checked my sight lines and then removed the BB pistol from its holster (on the side of the gas tank) with my left hand. Then I swiveled and fired at the line of cars. Two of the three windshields cracked, and the drivers veered off onto the shoulder of the road, but the third windshield held. I fired the remaining shots in the clip and then threw the empty gun at the pursuing car, as that car, the third car, came up alongside me. We were travelling, then, at the bike's top speed of just under fifty miles an hour. Lymphatico leaned out of the front passenger-side window, shouted something into the air, and then shot me in the ass, which knocked me clear off of the motorcycle, and sent me rolling onto a grassy embankment on the side of the highway. I ended up lying on my side, facing south. The southbound cars and motorcycles streamed away from me - and I found that I couldn't really think of them or of anything, but then, in the confusion, I saw my motorcycle. Though I had been knocked cleanly off it, it had continued along, upright on its path, for some distance, until it began to slow and wobble: then it gently laid itself down on its side and stalled. This was the last thing I saw before I lost consciousness. It was good to see that the bike had done well and had made it. We would ride again. Lymphatico had made a critical mistake. We would come for him.

THREE

The motorcycle is a collection of a thousand things about to fall apart. Countless systems that are ready to come undone. In the early days of owning my bike, I would inspect it each day, after riding, and discover that, each day, something new was missing. I had to remove almost every single (remaining) nut, screw, and bolt, over the entire surface of the bike, coat them all with thread sealant, (add in lock washers) and return them to their original positions. I did all of this carefully, for if you stripped a screw, or broke a component, there was no clear path as to where the replacement part would come from: it might not come at all. It was best not to break things.

It could possibly be said that the motorcycle consisted of low grade parts, that is was a poorly made Chinese bike, a cheap knock-off of another company's much stouter and more famous standard in the world of small motorcycles. That could possibly be said, but I would never say it, as I loved the bike dearly, then, as I still do, now.

I have always had a fondness for poorly made goods. I have a strong love of all things badly designed. When I purchase things, I seek out models and designs that were intended to be used only briefly, by the lowest rung of consumers, and then discarded. Products so cheap that the inherent cheapness of the item itself cannot be hidden through any ad campaign or packaging - to the point that the manufacturers often don't even try. That is what I enjoy. That is what I seek out.

I love nothing more than to purchase cheap, low grade items, and then sustain them with sheer love and determination far beyond their maker's expectations. Beyond the expectations of everyone. I find great joy in radically extending the useful life of things barely deemed useful to begin with. There is tremendous satisfaction inherent in keeping small things, such as inflatable pools, going year after year, lovingly patched with the strongest of industrial adhesives. There is true joy in this. For when I repair things, I remember the sense of play inherent in all things. And it is that sense of play that I must now focus on. It is that sense of play that I cannot now afford to lose, as I am sick and embattled, and I must admit that at times, too often, perhaps, I am in danger of losing sight of the lightness inherent in things. But the reparation of things returns me to it. It returns me to the light. When I fix things that are broken, there is a healing. A healing of both the object and myself. It is the manifestation of love for the object in front of me. I am buoyed up by the repair of simple material goods: I am made happy by returning the *good* to the *material*. As there is something terribly sad in broken objects that may no longer be used for their intended function. To return that functionality feels to be of the divine.

FOUR

The small motorcycle was the pinnacle of all this. The American company that had imported it from China had only been in existence for a brief time, and had in fact failed, before I even purchased the motorcycle, brand new, from a local store that had only the one - with no more available or on the way. The company's failure had lowered the asking price, increased the questionable quality of the motorcycle itself, and ensured that obtaining parts would be highly difficult, at best. In addition, it was bright, bright yellow. It was perfect. I could not have purchased it faster.

I keep a gun holster bolted to the side of the bike's stem, just below the seat, on the side of the gas tank. It holds a .177 caliber BB gun with a 19 shot removable clip and I maintain a fresh CO_2 cylinder just in case. You can fire the BBs as fast or as slow as you choose to pull the trigger. It is sometimes helpful to have.

I pack a gray motorcycle cover in the basket on the front of my motorcycle, as cover is another thing that is always good to have.

[I should be clear. As I have said before, I was never a beat cop on the south side of Chicago. I have never been a cop. But I would have liked to have been, at one time. It never worked out. I didn't gain the weight I needed, and I worried that I was too different from what I researched to be the personality of a standard police officer. I worried that I would not have the trust of whomever was assigned to me, to be my partner. I live now at the northern tip of Massachusetts and travel mostly in my mind.]

The basket contained a motorcycle tarp, with bungee cords, so that the bike could be covered and concealed if I ever had to abandon it in the forest overnight. The storage compartment on the back of the bike had a full set of tools, such that any mechanical repair I had ever previously performed I would be able to re-create on the road. In a separate bag, next to the tools, I kept an assortment of all the small parts most likely to fail or fall off. I had a full set of all the bike's light bulbs, along with a variety of bolts and locknut washers (all sizes), in addition to sparkplugs and magnetic emergency lights. It was also extremely important for me to carry at least one piece of fresh fruit. In addition, I carried some pain medications, some bandages, a small flask of hard alcohol, typically gin, a small bag of marijuana, and an extra fully loaded BB pistol, with a hip holster, in case things got hairy.

[As I have already indicated, I made a strong attempt to keep a piece of fresh fruit packed in - most commonly an orange. Although, this was not always possible. There are always wonderful things to be said for apples, and some of the other major fruits. I have been brought back across vast distances of solitude and loneliness many times through the strong draw of a good piece of fruit. I also made a point of trying to always leave room for a proper stand-alone bag lunch. And last but not least, there was always the unknown variable of any evidence that may be discovered and collected over the course of an investigation. I always tried to keep a little extra space for all the unknown madness that might come along.]

FIVE

There were times when the motorcycle had trouble. Sometimes it would stall incessantly at stop signs. I would shift down to first, as I pulled up to a sign, and with only a second's hesitation it would die on me. It could sometimes take up to 15 seconds to get it going again, as I struggled to get the right choke setting, based on how cold the engine was. All the while, thick waves of shame and anxiety would wash over me, as lines of cars gathered, with the drivers around me unsure on how to proceed - faced with the sad spectacle of a man who could not operate his motorcycle. But I would always get it going again, after some struggle, and then tear off through the intersection. It could take a number of miles, after such an incident, for me to regain my composure, but eventually the engine and my heart would both begin to warm, until it was almost as though they fused together. The motorcycle and I would soon move as one entity, traversing cracked and pitted, bumpy roads, dodging crippling gaps and holes, slaloming from one side of the road to the other in a fraction of a second, with only the slightest physical shift of weight, as though it were really just the mind itself rocketing us forward - effortlessly.

We were often out hunting - the motorcycle and I - on missions that we could not fail.

~

Sometimes though things went very poorly indeed. A few

weeks after my initial injury, I was out on my motorcycle, when a car that I thought was full of Cancertalkerous's men rapidly pulled up next to me (on the road) and brushed against me. I retrieved my holstered gun from the gas tank, and fired at my attackers. The side view mirror of the car caught my arm, the motorcycle went out from under me, and I rolled along the side of the road to a stop. The driver of the car then pulled over. But, it had not, in fact, been a gang attack, the driver was a young distracted mother who had brushed against me while texting.

I had inadvertently shot out the driver-side windows of a small passenger car, driven by a civilian, while I had been attempting to stop Cancertalkerous's men. The driver was a young woman who had two children on booster seats in the back of her car. I picked the motorcycle up from where it had fallen, turned off the engine, and hobbled over to the storage compartment at the back, where I struggled to open it with trembling hands. Once I'd gotten the key in the lock and turned it, I opened the lid and removed a small roll of hundred dollar bills, held together by an elastic. I then slowly approached the window of her car, and reached in, through the broken window frame, to gently place the roll into a (breast) pocket on her blouse. The woman was uninjured but catatonic, and she stared forward, with her hands still on the wheel. I crouched down to better assess all the occupants of the vehicle, and then I spoke, "My apologies, madam. I have struck two of your windows, but you and your children have not been directly injured. When you have recovered, take your vehicle to the repair shop listed on the business card that I have placed in your pocket, at the center of the roll. The owner of the shop is a friend of mine and he will take care of you. And I have a piece of fresh fruit for your children."

I then rummaged through my storage compartment, took the day's fruit from its container and addressed the child closest to me, "I'm afraid today's fruit is a tomato. Normally, it would be an orange or an apple, but tomatoes are still technically a fruit, and it is good for you."

The tomato was moderately damaged. The child did her best, I think, not to cry, but when I placed the tomato gently on her lap, she could not help but cry a little. "Wait," I said, "I think I might have one more thing."

I wasn't sure that I still had any with me, but it turns out that I did, in fact, have one small bag of glow-in-the-dark stars, hidden under some wrenches. I brought the bag of stars to the first girl and poured half of it into her outstretched hands. She was not able to smile outright, but she accepted them and stopped crying. Then, I went around the back of the car and poured the second half of the bag into the other child's hands.

I started to turn, to get back onto my motorcycle, when the young woman behind the wheel suddenly spoke to me, "He's still out there, you know."

"I know," I said. I returned to the storage compartment and pulled out the spare pistol, charged and loaded, still nestled in its holster, and I handed the whole thing to the young mother.

"Be well," I said. She nodded, and I turned and got back on the bike, started it up, and headed slowly back towards home.

I know sadness.

I know it as well as I know joy.

That is the big fear, isn't it? That we know (or we will know) more sadness than joy. That is the fear.

They are both present. You may know them both.

Do not be discouraged.

SIX

Before all this, I was a patient man. My name is Out Patient, but everyone calls me "Hors." I picked up the name when I worked in New Orleans for a few years after the disaster. I was part of a patrol sent to try to restore people's faith in the use of superdomes, after the dome horrors of Katrina. To be honest, I don't know that we succeeded. I feel sometimes that the people have not recovered from all the damage that was done. Regardless, my friends in The Quarter started calling me "Hors" because it's French for "Out" (I think). It had a certain ring to it, so I went with it. And it stuck, even after I returned to northern Massachusetts.

I don't know French well, but it is my understanding that they called me Hors perhaps because it meant "outside of" or "except for." I have always tended to work on the outskirts and edges of systems, as those are the only places that I have ever felt comfortable - New Orleans was no exception. I worked as closely as I could with the people, without actually forming lasting bonds. It bothered me that, in the end, our team was unable to restore faith in the larger systems. I think I held out longer than the others in wishing it to be so. On some level, I still, even now, have faith in the systems, and I wish for others to share this. Though it is not to be. Perhaps that is why they called me Hors, as I was one of the last holdouts, one of the last ones to give in. Regardless, it stuck, and that is what they now call me.

I am a patient man, but I am running out of patience. I am moving through the darkness now, shifting into position, preparing to strike.

~

I drove past The Lineman on my way to the hospital. He had been deployed to a bend in the road, at the edge of the woods, and was raised in the outstretched arm of the machine. He was raised up to the height of the trees, and was figuring the ins and outs of all the cabling before him.

He was focused on the mechanics of the moment, as he needed to be. While I was focused on leaning the bike down as low to the ground as I could (as I rounded the bend, below him) and so we simply nodded to each other as we passed.

The Lineman worked in conditions that were similar to mine. He labored to protect and serve the people. To provide them with power. He worked, as did I, with deadly variables. There was little tolerance for error. We both had to proceed forward with clear and sound judgment, at all times, as a simple error or mistake could cause the whole thing to fall apart.

SEVEN

When I am on the motorcycle, I drive it at the maximum speed possible at all times, though I constantly adjust for the conditions and objects around me. If there is a car on the road in front of me, and I am capable of catching up to it, I will make a rapid full-speed approach towards it, but then, upon the final approach, I will downshift and maintain a rigid distance of four seconds, regardless of how fast the car is travelling, until the car and I part ways. Unless, of course, I am hunting prey.

In order to allow yourself time to react to anything that may occur (and now is certainly not the time to forget that, indeed, anything may occur) you must maintain a distance of three to four seconds between yourself and the vehicle in front of you. The idea is that if something catastrophic happens, you will have that many seconds to deal with the situation. It is easy to tell at any moment how much reaction time you have allowed yourself. All you must do is pick a stationary object on either side of the road and begin counting in "Mississippi's" *the moment* the vehicle in front of you passes the object. When you yourself pass the chosen object, you will know how many seconds of reaction time you have allowed yourself. If, when you perform this test on your own, you discover that you only have one or two seconds of reaction time allowed to you, there is a significant risk, though I hate to say it, that you may be driving like an asshole. (It would be a shame to navigate the dangers of cancer and all of the world's other troubles only to die in a car accident.) Initially, I was going to tell you that it is far more likely that you would die in a car accident, than it is that you would ever die from cancer. I was going to say that to you. But I am afraid that I have recently researched the matter and found it not to be so.

So I may not speak on it.

Check in with yourself before you wreck yourself: adjust your distance to three to four seconds, in order that you may survive and prosper - as that is something I greatly wish for you to do.

~

I maintain an adjustable-death-grip when I am riding on the motorcycle. I move and adjust my hands in minor increments frequently, almost constantly, but in between movements my hands are locked around the grips as tightly as possible, the ends of my thumbs and forefingers pressed together in the shape of the Buddhist Mudra. Through this I am able to maintain my hold on the bike as it crashes and bounces through countless holes, divots, bumps and faults in the road. Jarring events both seen and unseen, expected and unexpected. Countless moments, testing, always testing, to see if the rider may be unseated. We are always testing to see if the rider will be thrown from his mount. But it is I who shall remain through the turbulence.

It is I who shall ride forth against sickness and the night.

EIGHT

This is how it went. This is how the story began.

I woke up in the hospital after a bad colonoscopy.*

Lymphatico had done a good job of messing me up. The bullet had gone into my colon and fragmented into my liver. The attending physician explained this to me (watching me closely) for my reaction. The bullet, and its fragments, would need to stay where they were for now, but I would eventually need massive surgeries to remove them. I nodded when he had finished speaking, and then I said, "You know we're going to need to get me a medical marijuana card." He laughed nervously at this, so I repeated it, slowly and clearly, and with that, he left the room.

*I woke up with stage four of the four stages of cancer. (There are only four stages in total.) I had somehow missed stages one, two, and three, but four had gotten my attention. I had colon cancer that had spread to my liver. It is a simple fact that once cancer has spread it is not usually curable. It is not something that is normally overcome. Of course, that didn't mean that we weren't going to overcome it. It didn't mean that we weren't going to fight it. No, dear reader, we were going to fight it. I just thought that perhaps you should know how it was.

I set out to find the one man that could help me battle Melonomames's gang. I had been told that he was an older Asian gentleman, named Mr. Chemagi. He'd been the leader of the cytotoxic agents during the war. The rumor was that if I could find him, and if he accepted me into his order, I would have a chance.

I knew someone who could point me in the direction of Chemagi. A German immigrant named Handsfull who tracked down hard to find resources for the hospital. I found him in the hospital's basement supply room, which he also used as an office.

It was a terrible office. It was a small windowless room that shared a wall with an adjoining grief room. I could hear the wailing of a woman, next door, when I arrived. Handsfull was coiling intravenous tubing around a wooden spindle. A bare light bulb swung slightly on a cord above him. "So, Mr. Patient, I have heard that you are not so well. You have danced with Melonomames's foot soldiers, no?"

"Call me Hors," I said. "I'm a patient man, but I'm running out of patience. I need help getting to Chemagi."

"Okay, Hors. I know of Mr. Chemagi," Handsfull said. "I do not know though if you are ready to see him."

NINE

Handsfull had first dealt with the gang years before when he had a run-in with Lymphatico. Lymphatico had killed Handsfull's golden retriever over a misplaced order of biscuits. I had read up on the case, and it was clear that the gang was responsible, but they'd intimidated witnesses and nothing came of it.

"Hands," I said. "I know you miss your *Golden*. They won't stop. He won't stop, unless I chase them all down and kill them. I need to get to Chemagi first."

"You realize, Hors, that they are no mere gang. They are dividing and replicating, all the time. They are proliferating around us, right now. They have become militarized. You are not facing Melonomames's *gang*. You are facing his *army*. How do you say, 'the odds are not very good?' I do not know why, but you Americans seem to enjoy this sort of thing. It is no matter, I will help you."

And with that, Handsfull picked up a King Cake off of a shelf behind him and held it before me. "There is magic in festivals and rituals. Do you remember your visit to New Orleans? Behold, the traditional Three Kings Cake of Carnival. You know, Mr. Patient, that the recipient of the "Trinket" inside the cake is subject to certain privileges and obligations, which I will not go into here. But, I digress, this particular King Cake is very special. Observe."

Hands pressed down on the center of the cake and a secret compartment swung open on the bottom, revealing what appeared to be a surgical knife.

"It's beautiful," I said.

"It is no mere scalpel," Hands said. "It is The Trinket of Trinkets. Observe the silver baby on the handle. With it, you may be able to cut out the heart of Cancertalkerous Melonomames. He may die. Take it, along with this carrying case, to avoid injury. Now, you must go. Chemagi will meet you at the loading dock behind the hospital a little after 4 pm. Godspeed, Mr. Patient."

I left the hospital through the backdoor with the trinket scalpel strapped to my leg. The carrying case was sleek and allowed for this. The handle, with the silver baby on the end, was highly polished and it caught the sun, glinting to the heavens. I was walking at a decent pace, heading for home. I'd read that walking is one of the best exercises you can do, and I'd made a pact with myself to do more of it, as part of my bid to stay alive.

Some hipsters with fancy gear brushed past me on my right. They were running at a good clip.

Joggers.

They were pounding their bodies into the ground, but they didn't even know it or care. "Assholes," I murmured under my breath, as they brushed my side. Perhaps I'd become more judgmental. (I have heard that such things are common with the onset of chronic illness.)

There was time to kill, and I had some errands to do before I met up with Chemagi. I had to stop at home, as there was a hungry old fish I needed to feed.

TEN

Ampoule was a nine-year-old South American Oscar. A type of cichild from the Amazon. I'd raised that fish since it was an inch-and-a-half long, as a baby. Now it was more than a foot long, weighed a few pounds, and was a tough old bastard. They say that Oscars are the dogs of the fish world. They follow you with their gaze when you step in the room, and they're one of the most intelligent fish that you can fit in a tank. It was all true. Ampoule was a good fish and she'd helped me on cases before. People sometimes asked me why I named her Ampoule and the answer was simple. Nine years before, on the day she'd arrived, I had some shopping to do beforehand, and I'd had a package of light bulbs in the cart. As far as the French, it just seemed right.

I made the final approach to the house through the woods that run along the edge of my property. I stood in front of my house, by the road barrier at the end of the street, hidden among the trees, where the dirt and ivy lead down to the ravine that runs behind everything. There's a stream at the bottom of the ravine that leads to the northern states. They say that coyotes and wolves run there in the night. I stood a while and listened, watching the pine trees that rose up, up ten stories above me - far older and wiser than I. They were beautiful - both full of motion and still at the same time. Then it was time to go. I turned and made my way into the backyard, checking the street first to confirm that I wasn't being watched.

I stepped into the house through the back door. I could already tell that there would be a lot of going in and out of back doors before this was all over. I said hello to Ampoule and fed her a superworm, along with a few pellets. Sometimes she had trouble locating the superworm on the surface of the water, as she was getting older, but this time she snapped it right up. It always made me smile when she didn't have trouble, and I complimented her on her good work.

As I was getting ready to go back to the hospital my phone rang. It was one of my old partners, The Humanist. He was from the mid-Atlantic region and he'd been kicked off the force due to his involvement in a complex sting. The sting had revolved around a mythical pasta-based creature known as the Flying Spaghetti Monster, or The FSM. The Humanist was a Pastafarian who'd been prosecuted for his lack of beliefs. The whole thing didn't smell right and the troops on the ground who kept their feet straight still stayed in touch with him.

"Hors," The Humanist said. "How are you holding up?"

"I'm all right," I said. "What have you got for me?"

"Before you see Chemagi, you need to see The Tortoise," he said.

He was right, of course.

"Thanks," I said. "I'm on it."

The Humanist ended the conversation the way he always did those days, by invoking the FSM, "May His noodly appendage touch you," he said.

"May it touch you as well," I said, and hung up.

I headed back outside, on my way to see The Tortoise.

Dr. Casing was an older top-notch colorectal surgeon, who maintained an office with a panoramic view, on one of the upper floors of the hospital, so that he could see things coming. He was thorough and normally proceeded slowly and methodically, but he had a real edge and could quickly be biting when necessary. He had the strength and ferocity of a snapping turtle, but he tended to stay calm and on the land, so everyone on the force called him The Tortoise.

A nurse led me back to his office. After very brief pleasantries, we sat down and he asked me about my symptoms. I went over the details that I knew and started to put in my perspectives, adding in insights I'd picked up along the way. But The Tortoise stopped me abruptly each time, guiding us back to the sheer facts. I was thrown by this at first, but I quickly began to see that he was processing the raw data on a higher level. He was good, and I was starting to learn that this process, many of these processes, perhaps, would not always be intuitive or clear to me, so I sat back and I went with it. The view from his office was, in fact, beautiful.

ELEVEN

We covered the verbal aspect of things, and then it was time for The Tortoise to pay a visit to the scene of the crime. He led me into an examining room partway between his office and the nurse's station, and then stepped out for a moment. I put the contents of my pockets on a silver tray, along with the scalpel from Handsfull and its scabbard and strap. Then I changed into a hospital gown behind a screen. When the doctor returned, he called out to his nurse, as he was closing the door, requesting the preparation of a specimen jar.

He then turned to me and saw the scalpel among my possessions on the tray. He took it out of its sheath without a word and held it up to the light. Turning it slowly in his hand, he gauged its weight and dimensions, and then laid it back down on top of the strap and scabbard. He looked directly at me when he spoke, "You have friends in high places, Mr. Patient. That is no ordinary blade. It is, in fact, extraordinary." I nodded solemnly and then he directed me to lie on the examination table.

As I started to get up on the table, there was a loud commotion from the nurse's station. We both turned as a gunman in black leather kicked open the door and rushed in. He had a pistol fully extended in his hands and he paused for a fraction of a second, searching for his target. Things slowed down and I heard the hammer cock, as though it were a faraway wet sound. Like a coin dropped into a well. The gunman, to his own detriment, seemed only to see me, and paid no attention to The Tortoise. It is always a mistake to ignore The Tortoise. The doctor picked up my scalpel from the silver tray and brought it down without pause, in a single powerful arc that severed several of the gunman's fingers. The gun clattered to the floor. Fingers fell softly around it. The man screamed and ran out of the room. We could hear him bumping into the walls along the corridor - struggling to find an exit - and an alarm began to ring in the distance.

"No one Fucks with The Tortoise," I said, bowing my head in deference. "Thank you."

He smiled at me briefly and then called out to the nurse's station as he cleaned the blade of the scalpel with gauze. "Mary, we're going to need additional specimen jars." Then he closed the examination door and we went through the business of the examination. At the end, he said, "You may get dressed. It's likely that that was in fact one of Cancertalkerous Melonomames's men. We'll run labs on the fingers to be sure. In the meantime, try to get some rest. I understand you've already made arrangements to meet with Chemagi?" I nodded and The Tortoise stepped out of the room, while I gathered my clothes and possessions, and then I made my way down to the lobby.

TWELVE

I made it to the loading dock, by the dumpsters, slightly after four. The whole area was deserted. The sun was beginning to set and the sky was starting to darken. A grayish-yellow light fell on the truck bays, and the alley leading up to them. The green dumpsters and the padding around the bays seemed to be turning brown in the light.

Something was fluttering by the entrance to one of the bays, so I climbed up onto the loading dock to inspect it. It was a pink adhesive page from a memo pad, pressed onto the wall. It was fluttering from the wind coming up the alley. I reached up to pull it off and it came loose before I could touch it. The note started to dive down towards the ground, away from me, and I grabbed at it - catching and crushing it, instinctively. I held it firmly in my hand for a second, before turning it over and un-crumpling it. This is what it said:

I'm here

But I am not here

I'll help

But I will not help you

I'll show you the path

But you must choose

To take it

You're not yet ready

You must meet first

With The Knights

They will lead you to me

Stop by the front desk

In the morning

It was signed "Chemagi." I folded the note over, placed it into my pocket, and began the walk back to my house.

~

I stopped at the library, along the way, to do some research on the cytotoxic agents.

As I was leaving the library, there were two girls sitting outside it on the stone steps, waiting for their mother. They smiled when I looked down at them, so I asked them what they were reading.

The older girl told me that she was reading a book about space and that it turned out that one million of our earths could fit into the sun. The younger one liked to be read to, but her favorites were the kind of books where you look for and then find things. I grinned at them, and told them that those both sounded like good subjects, and then I excused myself and headed down the stairs.

~

Sometimes, dear reader, I think, "What else do I need to

tell you? What else, do you need to know?" Of course, no matter what, I could never truly convey all that you will need to know. Or even a fraction of it. That is part of the cosmic joke, perhaps. But there is still a little more that I have for you. Do not give up on me, just yet, dear reader. You will figure out what you need to figure out, and the rest shall perhaps be a mystery wrapped around you. But there is something to be said for having mystery wrapped around you. It is not a bad thing. A little mystery can be delicious.

There will be many paths that you must choose, but you will (always) have what you need. Think of the following points, as you guide yourself:

1. Does it interest me? (If you must, on occasion do things that *do not* interest you, then you must look at those things again, as you do them - to find what is interesting about them - as there is always something intrinsically interesting in things. Find it. If it is not interesting, make it interesting.)

2. Am I somewhat scared of it? (Whatever it may be.) We are often most scared of that which threatens to draw us to the fringe of our creative capacities. There is often great work to be done there. Be brave and embrace it, you may be astounded by the magic that you find.

3. Be capable of protecting yourself. This is not a question. You must know how to kill a man (or a monster) and deploy that knowledge and power, as applicable, if it is called for. Sometimes a man and a monster can be one and the same. There is a time to gouge eyes and jam knees into groins, know this. Do not deploy it willy-nilly, but when it

is called for, do not delay. (Train for this.)

4. Have fun. (I have no annotated footnote or extrapolating comment for this - Have fun.)

5. Know that you are loved. You are, and you have been, and you will love and be loved again.

~

You may find, at times, that if feels like all the world's oceans are rising around you. Like all the port cities are under attack and disappearing. It may feel like the demands on your generation, are greater than the demands on the generations before you.

That it is all at risk of coming apart.

This may, in fact, be true. But do not be disheartened. It is often at the worst that we find our best. Band together, and with the remnants of society you may find that tremendous innovative inroads of survival are reached. Last minute cleverness may certainly come to pass, to hedge off disaster right as it is needed.

But, if it doesn't, that may be okay too.

Know that I love you.

THIRTEEN

I arrived back at my house after dark and made a cup of chamomile tea with honey. The hood over the stove had an incandescent bulb that cast its light onto the surrounding counters, where it dissipated into darkness.

I sat at a small green table in the sunroom, by the fish tank, to think about what was going on while I drank my tea. It was a good cup of tea. I owed this, primarily, I believe, to the honey, although it cannot be denied that the whiskey helped.

[Do not get me wrong, alcohol is very dangerous. You will need to find your own level with it, which perhaps is nothing at all. It can destroy you, if you're not careful. There are many dangers on our paths. You must learn what you can do, and what you cannot, and travel between the two. Moderation is the best path for this particular element. Do not think that it comes easily. Anyone who drinks alcohol on a regular basis must constantly check in with themselves, to see how they are doing, as it is easy to get lost. This applies, in fact, to all drugs, but we cannot go into detail here on all aspects of everything. You will already know, on some level, if you are tackling something tricky. If you are, you must face it head on. There is no guarantee that you will succeed, but there is a chance that you might, and on that chance alone you must proceed - as that is really the basis of this entire story, if you think about, it is all about proceeding on a chance, no matter how small, for all the good and ill that that entails. Be brave and you shall do well, regardless of what happens.]

I must admit that I am often not brave myself, and I must remind myself that being brave is not about proceeding forward without fear. Being brave is about proceeding forward even though you are filled with fear. There can be no bravery without fear. We move forward despite the things in our way, and somewhere, in there, is where the magic lies.

We must each do the best we can at being brave, and things, I'm quite sure, shall turn out well.

That being said, there is perhaps nothing more delicious and satisfying than a cold light beer, quickly consumed, when you are hot and tired and partially dehydrated, having just finished exerting yourself physically in some way - the electric carbonation of the beer slightly stinging your mouth and throat as you feverishly drink the majority of the drink without pausing to breathe or lower the can.

This can be as wonderful as a pomegranate.

But it may not be for you.

FOURTEEN

Things had progressed too far without a diagram. I keep a
thick pad of multicolored construction paper, of a high
grade, on hand at all times in my home. Construction
paper will never let you down as a reliable medium to build
a model or sketch something out on. It has solved crimes
and swayed juries. I tore off a yellow sheet and brought it
to the dining room table to begin. I drew a large capital "I"
in the center of the page and circled it. This would
represent myself. I was going to be at the center of this, no
matter how it turned out. I then began drawing lines out
to: Handsfull, The Tortoise, The Humanist,
Cancertalkerous Melonomames, Lymphatico, The
Gunman at the hospital, and to the most recent unknowns,
Chemagi, and The Knights.

At some point you have to acknowledge where a two-
dimensional pen can travel no farther, and be willing to go
to the next level. I cut out a graphical representation of
each character, using different colored papers, until I had
the whole cast so far. Then I glued them on - adjusting a
few as they dried - to get them right. Now we were in
business. The next step was to lower the diagram carefully
along the wall, behind the fish tank, so that Ampoule
could see the chart to give her input. Once I had it in
place, I pinned the edges to keep it there.

The Tortoise was green and traditional in his shape.
Handsfull was brown and shaped like a dog. The Gunman
was black, in the shape of a hand with missing fingers. The

Humanist was silver and shaped like the emblem for the Flying Spaghetti Monster. The Knights were white and shaped like a knife - I would meet them tomorrow - but Chemagi and Melonomames were question marks. I did not know what either one looked like, and knew very little about them in general. I had never seen Melonomames, and I had never seen Chemagi. Melonomames was, for now, a red cloud. Chemagi was a cloud of blue. They looked strange and ethereal there on the yellow diagram. But it was all I had for now, and it would have to do.

I have not mentioned the "I." For myself I cut out a red eye. I would be the eye at the center of the storm. A center of calm, surrounded immediately on all sides by turmoil. An eye of calm and watchfulness.

Of course, I had forgotten to put Ampoule on the chart, and she took notice of this right away - dashing back and forth in the tank. I quickly cut the fish's shape out of an orange piece of construction paper and taped it the best I could onto the diagram. I could have used the glue, but it might have run. My hand landed, in the small space between the aquarium and the wall, over the symbol of the eye. It appeared that the paper fish was swimming haphazardly across the eye. Ampoule noticed this and quickly came to stop in front of her symbol. She studied the paper eye and the paper fish, and swayed her body sideways, back and forth, as she thought about it.

Having studied her own presence on the diagram, she began slowly scanning the remainder of the sheet, pausing on each icon as she moved across the tank.

I stepped out to let her work. I turned off all of the

downstairs lights (except for the fish tank's) and made my way upstairs in the dark. I stopped in the bathroom to brush and floss before heading off to bed. (I didn't actually brush or floss, but I should have.) I made my way to the bedroom, carrying a few cans of beer, in case I needed them, and lay down on top of the comforter. I was tired, but did not sleep well. I was calmly awake, then I was calmly asleep, then I was calmly awake again (with a desire not to get up). In the end, I decided to sit in bed, until I saw the sun, in the morning.

~

The nights were frequently long and difficult.

There are subtle biological and social guidelines that quietly whisper to you in your wakefulness that you should be asleep. The very night has been set aside for this. The night is your one real chance to heal and to rest, as there is rarely time for such things during the day. (In addition, there are implicit and explicit healing instructions which clearly insinuate that the possibility of getting better is intrinsically tied to how well you are able to rest.) The pineal gland, in your brain, the very regulator of sleeping and wakeful cycles, itself, calls out to you silently.

Why are you not asleep?

In a way, the simple act of sitting up awake all night, itself, can seem to portend doom. Just the simple act of being awake when you are not supposed to be, can make you feel as though you are rocketing towards you own end. It is hardest to be resolute and hopeful in the stillness of the night. It is hardest to see yourself through to the other side of chronic illness, as you sit through hundreds and hundreds of consecutive minutes of darkness.

And then, of course, there is the larger question of whether or not you are going to make it.

You can surround yourself with friends, family, loved ones and caregivers. They may surround you, and tend to you, buoying you up (during the day) but even they must sleep and rest.

It is then, in the heart of the night, when all others are asleep (when you are too distracted to be absorbed by your own distractions) that you must face things down and come to terms with them.

There's something to be said for taking drugs, on occasion, too.

FIFTEEN

I have never enjoyed the business of food preparation. So I kept it simple in the morning, with a bowl of hempen cereal, a glass of coconut water, and some gummy vitamins. I was due that morning to meet with The Knights to discuss my prognosis and where things were going.

I had recently picked up an English walking stick that had a hidden compass and a small corked flask, tucked away in its spine. I filled the flask with the best gin I could find in the kitchen, repacked it, and prepared to head out. I didn't need the walking stick yet, but I liked the idea of training with it, getting used to it. It was constructed of hard wood, with a solid brass handle. It had a good reach and a heft to it - it would be perfect for beating back rabid dogs, or smashing twisted gang members. And there was always the chance that I might get thirsty.

The morning air was brighter and lighter than it had been the day before. I had found a pair of large, dark, reflective sun glasses by the door and put them on. I was walking at a good clip, on my way back to the hospital, striking the end of the cane down decisively on the sidewalk as I went. The hilt of the Trinket of Trinkets was just concealed, on my right hip, beneath a flashy new blazer, which had been given to me by a local mother's group that was concerned for my health.

~

When I scan a room, or a street, for henchmen or foot soldiers, or, for that matter, for danger of any kind, I have developed a technique that I learned from look-and-find books. I parse each section of the room, or page, or street, and look for things that I am not looking for. Sometimes it is only once you have allowed your eyes to relax - when you have allowed yourself to give up a little - that the true shapes of what you are looking for come into play.

~

I spotted some of Melonomames's men at an intersection in front of the hospital. There were four of them in a low-rider that was stuck in traffic. I made my way to the island in the middle of the intersection and stood by their car. The driver lowered his window and motioned to the passenger next to him, "Excuse me, sir, but my friend here is looking for The Hand Service Unit. Do you know where it is?" As he looked up at me, he jiggled his hand over his lap in a mocking masturbatory way.

SIXTEEN

I looked at the young man sitting in the front passenger seat and saw that his left hand was heavily bandaged and resting on his lap. (The Hand Service Unit was, in fact, on the second floor of the building I was headed towards.) The driver and the two men in the back were all staring hard at me - staring through me it seemed - and I could see they all had pistols (real pistols) sticking out of their belts. I pulled my head back from the car a bit and surveyed the traffic. There was a marked police cruiser stuck in traffic several cars behind them.

"You're going to want to take a left here, and then go straight to Hell," I said to him. I shifted my cane from my right hand to my left, and I slipped my right hand under my blazer, pulling The Trinket of Trinkets out from its sheath, where I held it hidden against my side.

The driver reached for his gun, but the traffic light above him had turned green while we were talking, and the cars behind him, including the police cruiser, began honking. I leaned in close to the car, pressing and holding the knife against the gorgeously painted flourishes on the car door.

"You'd be wise to go," I said. The driver looked at me with a raging hatred then returned his hands to the steering wheel and proceeded through the intersection. I kept the blade, hidden by my blazer, pressed against the car as he drove off, keying a deep gouge that undulated up and down, like a sine wave, along the length of his car. He must have heard the scraping sound because he jammed on the brakes in the middle of the intersection, causing the car behind him to rear-end him. Three of the four men in the low-rider jumped out with their arms in the air in outrage, and headed towards me. "What the fuck did you just do to our car?" one of them shouted, but by now the police cruiser, a few cars back, was in the intersection too – with the officers getting out to process the scene, and Melonomames's men quickly became subdued, got back into their car, and fled.

I probably should have stayed and dealt with things, but you have to pick your battles. I put The Trinket blade away, returned the cane to my right hand, and quickly crossed over the remainder of the intersection: disappearing into the matrix of hospital buildings beyond.

SEVENTEEN

The Knights were ready for me. There were three of them, and they met with me simultaneously. I had been led, by a receptionist, into an unusual waiting room that had a vast array of forest vegetation. There were a large number of ferns spread around the room. Lichen grew over the edges of the counters, and there seemed to be small clusters of deciduous and coniferous trees rising together in bundles, all around the room. The receptionist left and closed the door behind her, and I had trouble finding where the door had been. There was a rustling in the bushes, several small snakes passed along the floor before me, and then a bird took flight, soaring up into the canopy of trees over my head, where it settled in some branches. At that moment, the three Knights stepped out from behind a tree. One was a man and the other two were women. They were all wearing some sort of full-body plated armor, which looked old and medieval, and I could not make out their faces, as they had on helmets with visors. The three of them stood silently, for a moment, in a row, and I considered them there before me in the dappled forest light. They raised their right arms, with their palms facing out towards me, and chanted forcefully in unison, "Do No Harm!" and then they removed their helmets, which they held down at their sides. The man then addressed me, "Good Morning, Mr. Patient. We are The Knights. You may call me Dr. Aspen. And these are my fellow Knights, Dr. Birch, and Dr. Spruce. The solution, in the end, will come from the forest and the trees."

Dr. Aspen held the Staff of Asclepius at his side. An ancient golden rod with a serpent entwined around it.

"Your uniforms are unconventional," I said.

Dr. Aspen looked down at his armored suit and touched a large dent in the breast plate with his thumb.

"Ah, yes," he said. "We have been fighting cancer a long time, my friend." He then looked at me steadily. "Our fight is an old fight. As old as time. We have not just come to this, I'm afraid. We have been fighting a long while. We wear these plates and chains to remind us, from where we have come."

"We wear this garb," Dr. Birch, the woman standing next to him said, "To remind us of strides we have made."

"And that we have yet to make," Dr. Spruce, the woman standing on the end, added.

"I see," I said.

Dr. Spruce then spoke again, "You are young. You may be able to beat Cancertalkerous. We will champion your cause. You must begin a strict regimen - to train to be able to meet him in battle. You must follow Chemagi, and do as he says. Then we will ride into battle with you, and The Fates shall decide."

"Go now, your training begins in the morning," Dr. Birch said, and then she smiled at me. With that The Knights put on their helmets, turned and left the clearing.

EIGHTEEN

I decided on my way home to visit The Pilot. He hadn't flown in a long time - his eyes were going, and he hadn't kept up his hours, but he'd been a bush pilot, who'd been in the shit, back in the day. Now he mostly did consulting work, along with some side work on his two hobbies, bicycles and explosives. He'd done a lot of unregulated demolition work, as a teenager in the far north, and he still had a taste for it. And he'd always loved bicycles.

I arrived at his office door in the mid afternoon. Bright sun poured in, at a steep angle, through the large multipaneled windows behind his desk. The sunlight seemed to slow down and linger on the small dust particles suspended in the air, and then dissipate as it died out in the corners of his office, blocked in its path by the small totems and trinkets that lined the walls - talismans and figurines that he'd picked up in his travels around the world.

"Hors, it's good to see you," he said. "You're just in time for a cup of tea. Is peppermint okay?"

"Peppermint's just fine," I said.

The Pilot was standing by a small circular end table at the side of his desk, fiddling with a steaming teapot and some cups. He poured a small amount of the peppermint tea into a cup and breathed it in rapidly like a smelling salt. "It needs something," he said.

"May I?" I asked, raising my cane in question.

He nodded, and I unscrewed the top, revealing the hidden vial of gin within. I uncorked it with my teeth, and poured it into the teapot. The Pilot swirled the teapot and then poured us each a healthy cup. We clinked our glasses together and then drained them. The tea was hot and satisfying and it burned in a variety of ways.

"That'll do it," he said with a wink. "Please, have a seat." And he motioned to a chair in front of his desk, while he himself settled into the chair behind it.

"I've heard about what happened to you, Hors, and I was sorry to hear it. I've had some good friends who got the same thing. Same thing, and I was sorry to hear it."

"What happened to them?" I asked.

The Pilot took a cigar out of his desk, lit it, and inhaled deeply. "They didn't make it," he said, and he looked away into the corner of his office, for a moment, then returned his gaze to me and continued. "But, you can't take this sitting down, Hors. You've got to fight it! You've got to fight Him. Here's the way I see it. Cancertalkerous fucked up your ass. Now, you need to fuck Cancertalkerous in the ass! You'll need this..." and with that he pulled a brown paper bag out from a large drawer and dropped it heavily on the desk in front of me.

"What's in it?" I asked.

The Pilot bit down on his cigar and inhaled deeply. "It's filled with C-4. Made it myself. It's not regulation, but it'll blow the shit out of anything. What you need to do is find their headquarters. Find the nest, and blow their fucking asses across the street!"

"I will," I said.

"Good, good," The Pilot said, and then he rummaged around in his drawer, and produced another paper bag, which he placed gently on the desk next to the first bag. "Almost forgot the detonators and timers. Don't put 'em together until you're ready to party." And then he smiled and got up to pour himself another cup of tea.

"I'm going to ride for you in a bike charity, kid, to support the fight. Now get out of here, I've got some consulting work to do," and he smiled and winked again. I couldn't help smiling myself.

I thanked him, gathered the bags carefully, and then headed out.

NINETEEN

The rest of the afternoon was uneventful. I made my way home, had a quiet dinner and then sat outside, to think, on the deck behind the house. I had ten kerosene torches set out along the railings of the deck. The torches were attached with compression clamps that grabbed onto the wood of the deck, but the tighter the knobs were turned, the more they pushed themselves off the very wood they were trying to hold. They were poorly designed. They threatened to pop off at any moment - to push the burning torches to the ground. I loved them, but I would not allow this. I had drilled holes in the thickest part of the support plates, when I purchased them, and had attached them with deck screws - anchoring each firmly in place. The compression clamps merely acted as aesthetic complements.

I was sitting on the back deck, peering through the flickering torches, to the woods that rose from the ravine. I was thinking about the beginning of treatment with Chemagi, wondering what it would entail. The small frogs, the peepers, down in the ravine, called out to one another in the night.

I went to bed late and spent the night transitioning back and forth between waking and sleeping. In the morning I went to the hospital and checked in. I received a bracelet with my name and some other medical information, and was then led into an examining area. A technician took my vital signs and then released me back into the waiting area.

Some time passed and I was brought into a treatment room. I sat down on a large white leather chair and the volunteer who had brought me in stepped out and closed the door. I examined the room around me. It was a small square room with a good view of the city. There was a white speaker bolted to the arm of the chair, and as I settled in, the speaker clicked on, "Good Morning, Mr. Patient, It's so very nice to meet you."

"Good morning, Chemagi" I said. "I'm a patient man, but I'm running out of patience, call me Hors. What do we do now?"

"I am glad that it is not I who am running out of *patients*," Chemagi said, and laughed. "All we have to do now, Hors, is to have you battle Cancertalkerous Melonomames to the death. One of you will die. What do you say, sound fun?"

TWENTY

"I'll do what I have to do," I replied.

"I know," Chemagi said, "That is why you are here. That is why I have chosen to treat you. You are young, and you have the chance of a young man. It's going to be very exciting no matter how this ends. And now, we begin." And with that I heard Chemagi clap his hands over the intercom - the door to the treatment room opened and a tall, long-legged nurse in a short white skirt entered rolling a metal stand covered with intravenous bags and tubing.

It was time to begin.

The nurse began dancing seductively around the IV stand.

"What's with the dancing?" I asked.

"This is Rock Candy. She's a dancer at one of my clubs. She had a few semesters of nursing and pre-med, but it didn't work out. This is a treat, Hors. Consider yourself treated. Life is short. The real chemotherapy treatment is highly unpleasant and nauseating - we'll begin that shortly."

And at that moment, a more matter-of-fact looking nurse entered the room and began prepping me for the treatment - cleaning a site on my arm and then setting up the intravenous needle, while Rock Candy continued to dance wildly around her stand.

"It's important to start off right," Chemagi said. "And I think this balances the whole thing out."

I agreed with him silently.

Rock Candy finished dancing, the other nurse finished my preparations and then both left the room, and I was alone, with the exception of Chemagi on the intercom.

"So, Hors, let's take stock of where we are. You are currently experiencing the effects of stage four, of the four stages of cancer. It has spread from your rectum to your liver. What will it do beyond? We do not know. That is where I come in. I will subject you to a rigorous, no nonsense, full-blast treatment that will last months, if not years. In order to be effective, the treatment itself will be constantly in danger of crippling you further or killing you outright. We will weave in and out of major surgeries - replacing and adding parts - as needed. Then we will stop and take a look at you and see what we have - what we have left. Do you have any questions?"

"No," I said.

"Good," Chemagi replied, "Let's begin. We're starting you on a saline electrolyte solution to keep down the vomiting and then we'll move on to the hardcore drugs. You'll be on a rotating diet of at least a half a dozen anti-nausea medications, to keep things under control, and you will likely experience a wide variety of symptoms including tingling, pain, exhaustion, depression, involuntary muscle spasms, curling eyelashes, and an extreme sensitivity to cold."

The intercom was silent for a few moments, and then it crackled on again, "Oh, and I almost forgot, it's time for you to meet your new partner."

TWENTY ONE

The door to the treatment room opened, and a tall, dark, imposing man stepped silently through the doorway and stopped by my IV stand. He stood watching me with a raised eyebrow and I felt uncomfortable right away.

"Where did you come from?" I asked.

"From the forest. From the trees," he said.

"Hors, this is Irinotecan. He's Native American, I think. He's one of our best and strongest cytotoxic agents, and he's been assigned to you."

"You are sick," Irinotecan said to me, "I have seen this before. I will try not to wear you down and irritate you further, but things happen." And as he spoke, he grinned broadly.

I was processing this information when Chemagi chimed in, "Irinotecan can cause headaches, nausea, hair loss, poor appetite, flatulence, coughing, weakness and fever - and you will irritate each other no end, but I wouldn't trust your care right now to anyone else. No one has a better chance at interrupting all of the gang activity that's been rising up around us. Melonomames has been recruiting assholes left and right."

Irinotecan continued to grin at me, and I smiled back and nodded. I was going to say something, but my stomach had turned and I needed to excuse myself, as I suddenly realized that I needed to make it to the bathroom very quickly. I lurched into the hall, heading towards the restrooms, pulling my IV stand along with me, and Irinotecan began to follow. "Please," I shouted back to him, "I need to do some things alone." He nodded and stayed behind, as I pushed off furiously down the hall.

The treatment lasted all day, and it involved many pills and intravenous chemicals. I will admit that I was more thoroughly worn down and groggy by the end of it than I had expected. By the end, I wanted nothing more than to crawl into a corner and stay there. Irinotecan offered to drive me home, I accepted, and we walked outside to the hospital's parking garage together.

There were a couple of kids smoking cigarettes outside. We stopped in front of them, and watched as a car full of Cancertalkerous's men passed by the entrance to the hospital. After the car passed, I pulled myself up to my full height (the best I could) and walked directly up to the young smokers. "Listen," I hissed at them, "you keep on doing what you're doing and Cancertalkerous Melonomames *will come for you*. Know this. Good day."

Irinotecan then stepped forward and quickly grabbed the lit cigarettes right out of the mouths of the children. He flipped both the cigarettes around, popped them in his own mouth, and took a long drag. Then he shrugged his shoulders at them, and we turned away to enter the parking garage.

As we walked up the stairwell of the garage, to get to Irinotecan's car, smoke from his two cigarettes trailed behind us and I thought about pointing out that his methods seemed to be in danger of weakening my message, that it was going the wrong way, but in the end, I decided to let it go.

Luckily, when we reached the right floor, there was a trash barrel not far from the stairwell, and I was able to vomit into that before climbing into Irinotecan's car, where I fell into a dark and addled sleep.

TWENTY TWO

Treatment with Chemagi proceeded on, several days a week, for months. On the days that I had treatment, Irinotecan, or "Rinno," as I liked to call him, met me at the hospital and accompanied me. On the days I had off, I ran errands, visited people, and worked on the case.

Walking is certainly good. There is no question of that. But as the treatment went on, it became important for me to conserve what energy I had left, and so, more often than not, I rode my motorcycle whenever I could. I rode it on days when I had to travel to the hospital, or when I was running errands or visiting old friends. And on many days, I drove it with no destination. I drove it just to drive it. I drove it just to keep my heart light. To try and be free.

Riding the motorcycle home after sunset was always a tricky business. I stuck to the back roads as much as possible. The highways were dangerous, but the back roads were poorly lit, and equally as dangerous, as the bike didn't have much of a headlight. But it was always exhilarating, coasting around the sharp bends, leaning in, following the hazy edge of the road.

The taillight bulb needed to be replaced at least once a week, as all the slamming around on the pitted roads kept breaking the filaments. But light bulbs were always in good supply, as they were among the few simple parts that I could easily get, and I switched them out dutifully, as needed.

~

Napping is a dangerous drug for me. I am strongly drawn to it, and have immense trouble in breaking free from its grasp, once I am there. If I take a daytime nap (at any point during the day) I am often unable to break free until late, late in the evening.

It is fantastic to nap, but it risks destroying me entirely.

Napping is one of my biggest dangers. I am infatuated with the process of falling asleep. Once I have initially fallen asleep, I return again and again to the surface of wakefulness, but cannot compel myself to stay (there at the surface) and I dive down, again and again, into deliciousness.

When I do finally return to the waking world, it is only then because napping will no longer have me. I return only because I may, then, no longer sleep. I return, exhausted, and groggy, disoriented and depressed, pointed fully towards despair and desolation - with almost no chance of being able to sleep that night.

But, oh, if it wasn't fun getting there.

Napping is a drug for me. It is one of my biggest dangers.

TWENTY THREE

When I arrive at the hospital, I take the elevator to the seventh floor, to sign in for treatment. There are always hard candies available in the waiting room. I always recommend the brown and the yellow ones, as I find them to be the best. Though you may choose, when you get there.

You will want to know what it is like, because it is interesting. And so I will tell you. You arrive at the hospital at all different times of the day, but it always seems that you arrive early in the morning and leave late at night. After you prove your identity at the front desk, you may move to either side of the room, where you wait, alone or with your loved ones, for the time to pass. You are in a room, a waiting room, of people who are well on their way towards death. Or worse, they are in love with someone who is well on their way towards death. Most everyone is older than you. People are probably friendly and talkative, but there is no reason to talk to them. (We are not there to make friends, or to come to terms with things in a collective sense.)

When they finally call you, they check your name and your temporary medical bracelet a thousand times, and it is tempting to pretend that you are not that person. It is tempting to be funny and pretend that you are someone else entirely altogether. But to commit to that joke, you would have to be friendly both before and after the joke, and commit to follow-throughs and begin to learn names.

But it is quickly determined that it is not worth all that. That is not the corner into which you should put your energy. You have a small percentage chance of survival, and your energies are best spent on doing just that, on surviving. (We will chat and joke at the after-party.) You affirm your identity and are led into an examining room, where you wait a little more. Eventually you are weighed and estimated, and you are encouraged to state where you stand on the pain scale, and whether or not you feel threatened at home. A complimentary yogurt is offered at this time. The perfect side for this is a small cylinder of room temperature apple juice or ginger ale. When the doctors come in, the real crux of the discussion is how much weight you've lost and how tired you are, as these are the two real parameters that will tell them - more than any others - whether or not you will live or die. Of course, there's plenty of obligatory blood work and tests and scanning, but it all really comes down to these two questions. Then, of course, there is the matter of how you are actually doing. You're there, which is half the battle, but during treatment, as you're going through it, something happens. It is a slow and subtle process that I can best describe as this: you are a sealed hardwood floor at the beginning of the process, and as you enter into a prolonged sickness, the veneer that covers the surface begins to wear away - until the dull wood underneath is exposed. Weathered dirty wood that is susceptible to stains and scratching. Pitting and dents. You have come a long way from the majestic tree, from which you were cut. And it takes a long time to come back. Even after you are well. If you get well. To some degree, you will spring back naturally, regaining your natural sheen and imperviousness.

Stephen R Wagner

But it may also take a tremendous amount of drugs, both legal and illegal, to pump you back up to where you were. It will take a tremendous amount of time and luck to get rid of the side effects: the neuropathy, the discomfort, the achiness and the depression. The fear and the anxiety - it will take a while for these to pass. If, indeed, they do pass.

That is what it is like.

~

If you get cancer, you will find that you spend a lot of time in the cancer machines. Machines that scan and scan you to see if you have been infected. They are good and they are helpful. But do not forget, they are cancer machines. They both detect and make it.* You must use them in moderation. They function exactly on the line between sickness and health. It is a tricky business.

*My doctor has assured me that most of the machines do not make cancer.

Perhaps.

Perhaps.

Tread cautiously.

70

TWENTY FOUR

I was talking, once, with Chemagi, over the intercom, and I said, "He's pure evil, you know. I've got to stop him."

There was a pause, and then Chemagi replied, "Perhaps. But you do not know all that you think you do. The rumors are not all true, some of them are simply rumors."

"What do you mean?" I asked.

"Cancertalkerous Melonomames was once a good man, just like yourself." Chemagi said. "He had a wife and children. They had loving relationships. But his wife and children were killed (by radiation). They were killed and the experience mutated him as a man. Unending tides of anger and despair washed over him until the anger took root in his heart, where *it*, the very anger, became malignant and was able to reproduce and multiply. It spread throughout his core and took over the entire being. His very foot soldiers are physical manifestations of the original disease. Born healthy, they have been corrupted by him in their immaturity. They have lost sense of their own original purpose and now work blindly only for him. At least, so I have been told."

"He made a choice," I said. "I have made choices too. I could have gone into advertising. I understand people's brains, and I could have manipulated them with clever campaigns to buy things. But I did not do this, because to do so would have been wrong. I have decided, instead, to help. He, himself, had the chance to choose to help. Even when the sun and the planets themselves had turned on him, he should have resisted - though he did not. And now, I must call for him."

"You must defeat him in your heart and mind, before you (may) ever defeat him in a field of battle. He and his followers are sick, but they are strong. You must be sicker and stronger. It is no easy task, and you will likely fail, but I've enjoyed our time here together. I have enjoyed our little talks," Chemagi said.

And that was that.

TWENTY FIVE

Many people do not understand why I choose pellet guns and small engine bikes over proper guns and motorcycles. I will explain it briefly to you now. I am in touch with what I am comfortable with, and I have found things that match the exact levels of where I want to be. I am at equilibrium. Most people are uncomfortable with the level of where they are at. It is either too much or too little for them, but they are often uncomfortable saying so. I choose the pellet gun, as I may stop you with it (if you are an intruder) though it is highly difficult to outright kill someone with one by mistake. I choose the small engine motorcycle, because it goes fast enough to get where I need to go, without going too fast. In addition, I can wipeout on it, and (provided I don't hit an immobile object and that I'm wearing my full gear) I can stand up, get back on the bike, and head back into the mouth of danger. I have done this. I have done this more times than you know.

Part of what makes me unstoppable, is that I seem, at a glance, to be easily stoppable. Conclude so at your own peril. I have already drawn my semi-automatic, 19 shot BB pistol, while you were thinking about this, and I am deciding, with the muzzle extended, if I need to take an eye. (This is what you would face, were you on the side of darkness.) Remain in the light, or I will be obligated to hunt you too.

This is why I have been chosen. This is why the stones and the rocks and the plants have made me a warrior. Because

I know a secret. Though I will share it with you now. The trick to be a tremendous force of light and good that can transform the gods, the trick is not to *want* to be that force, but to simply *be* it.

TWENTY SIX

I always wear full gear when I ride, because I cannot afford to die before I am finished. The boots are steel toed. I have dragged them across the ground, many times, when the bike has come out from under me, but I have pitted them only mildly - to a depth of a quarter inch or so. Hence, the beauty of steel toes. I pop up, ready for action, at the end of the slide. The over-pants that I wear over my regular pants are made of a canvas/vinyl blend and are fitted with Kevlar knee-pads. I feel no scrapes, nor the touch of gravel, as I slide along the ground. The jacket is a professional, waist length, motorcycle jacket, reinforced in every way to brush off obstructions. The majority of the jacket is black, with a large yellow stripe at the center, and a lesser white stripe above. The white and yellow match the metal and plastic trim-work of the bike. The full face helmet is sturdy and bright yellow, with a clear visor that rises. I have hit my head on the ground with it only slightly, on occasion, and have thus preserved the protective core within. The gloves are black leather, and they fit perfectly, as they must. Lastly, the sunglasses have a yellow tint, as I find that there is a grayness that often tries to envelop me. A grayness that could always stand a little lightening.

TWENTY SEVEN

There are three rules for the shooting range in the basement. The first is that you *may* be drunk. The second is that you *must* wear safety glasses, even if you are only observing. The third is that you *may never* point a gun at another person, even in jest, even if you are sure that the gun is unloaded.

I stock a variety of weapons for the range, with members of both the BB and pellet families represented. There are spring piston guns, pump guns and guns that are powered with CO_2 cylinders. I shoot BBs and unleaded pellets only, as a piece of lead the size of a pencil eraser, ingested, is enough to slow the brain development of a child. The world does not need that. So I shoot only unleaded pellets, even though there have been many studies that show that they fly less straight and hit less powerfully than their more dangerous counterparts. I reflect on this in the following way: the forces of darkness upon which I am about to descend are fully unready for the wrath I am about to bring them. It is only fair for me to approach them severely handicapped, as I want them to think that they have a chance. And so, among the many advantages I give them, we add to these advantages the fact that my unleaded pellets are slower and less accurate than the leaded ones. I want them, *the forces I face*, to think that they have a chance. And then I will take *that, that chance*, away from them.

Of course, Melonomames and his entire gang used real

guns, and drove proper cars and motorcycles, which made the whole thing that much more exciting.

[Just to be clear, if you carry a pellet gun off of your immediate property, into public, and are seen by anyone, you will likely be shot to death by the police, in the confusion. I will not be able to stop this from happening. As I will not be with you. You must choose your adventures wisely, and understand the potential ends that the threads may lead out to. As I told you before, I, myself, have many connections, and I am able to pass through many doors that remain closed to others. I have, through circumstances that have evolved over time, been given certain liberties.]

It is highly probable that these liberties have not been granted to you.

TWENTY EIGHT

I had a jar of high-end un-pitted green olives, in a light brine, for lunch. We have gotten away from having things with pits. We have eschewed hard, dark centers - things that can break our teeth - if we are not careful of them. We have turned largely to processed, pitted things that have had their centers removed. It is important to understand that when the pit is removed, more is removed than the just the pit. The center is lost.

There is something to be said for the pit. I sit, at the bench in the park, and eat my un-pitted green olives greedily. It is a wondrous process to sink your teeth into the meat of the olive. Down just to the surface of the pit, no further, yet here the teeth probe - holding and turning - weighing the facts of the stone before them - and then they steal away all of the meat. I think of Melonomames's gang as I chew. I approach each member as my teeth approach an olive pit - carefully, carefully, carefully, until at just the right distance, we tear everything apart. We destroy it, ingest it and turn whatever it was into ourselves. We turn it into us - to power us further. We are nurtured off of its destruction.

The day was sunny and cool, and I drank the gin from my cane, as I ate, and felt refreshed.

~

I am having trouble keeping up with the algae inside the fish's tank. It quickly accumulates. It rises, a green opaque wall that I may not see through. A physical sign of my neglect. The fish begins to disappear, until it is completely hidden. Lost to me behind a verdant wall of sorrow. For long stretches it remains hidden. Long days pass when I can neither see it (the fish), nor the tactical board that festers somewhere behind the tank.

It is hard to always find the energy, and there are days when it simply is not found. Days when even important things are not done.

TWENTY NINE

One day, while we were sitting in the waiting room of the infusion ward, I handed The Trinket of Trinkets to Irinotecan. It was the special blade from the celebration of Three Kings, which The Tortoise, Hands, and I, had all thought could kill Cancertalkerous Melonomames. He took it carefully and turned it in his hand. He then looked up at me and spoke, "This is the mistake you make, my friend. This is a fine blade. It has no equal among the everyday blades currently made on this earth. But I have seen finer. Ten thousand years ago, before the introduction of horses and the invention of bows, men of the soil hunted large animals with rock-tipped spears, on foot. Look at your Trinket knife under a microscope, along with a stone knife from that era and compare the two. You will see one to be blocky and thick, with thick flaky layers, one shall be sleek, straight, sharp and fine." And then he added, "But, not as sharp as you, my friend." And then he released a deep and tremendous laugh that drew the attention of everyone in the waiting room.

I nodded to Rinno, as he returned the blade to me, and then I quickly made my way to the bathroom, as I felt a wall of nausea quickly rising around me.

I scurried away and Rinno called out to me, "They will not find the answer to truly beat Melonomames until they return to the plants, the roots, and the trees. That is where the answer lies. Where so much is hidden."

But I was around the corner by then, well on my way to the bathroom, and that was the end of the conversation.

~

Standing in the bathroom, looking into the mirror, after rinsing out my mouth and wiping down my face, I stopped and I said aloud, "We're going to need to smoke a lot more weed," and my reflection grinned, as we both nodded.

"Fishbowl the bathroom," I saw my reflection say.

"I can't," I said, "We're at the hospital and Rinno's right out there."

"Irinotecan is already as high as a kite, and they shouldn't have locked the door to the roof garden, if they didn't want you to smoke in here," my reflection replied.

My reflection had a point.

I took the kit out of my jacket pocket and then used my coat to block the space under the bathroom door. There wasn't a lot in the kit: a small lighter, and a small one-hit-bat designed to look like a partially smoked cigarette . It was fitted with a hollow tip - packed with just the right amount of marijuana. It was a metal cigarette, but the dimensions and the colorations mimicked a real cigarette very well. I could probably use it among civilians, out on the streets. I could probably even light it up in front of Cancertalkerous's own men, and they would be none the wiser.

I smoked quickly, in the handicapped stall, and then put my coat back on and the kit away in my pocket.

"Let's do this," I said to Irinotecan when I came out from the bathroom. We were soon admitted to a room, and I was hooked up for my four-hour session.

Just before I fell asleep on the hospital bed, as they pumped anti-nausea sleep inducing drugs into me, I told Irinotecan, "I will hand The Trinket of Trinkets over to the Tortoise and The Knights, as it may help them, in the coming battle between the doctors and the henchmen."

Rinno nodded, and then I was out.

THIRTY

I don't drive a car. They won't give me handicapped plates.
I looked into the paperwork required to get them, and it
turns out that I'm not disabled enough. Although
sometimes I feel pretty disabled. But, as I said, I looked
into it and losing your rectum doesn't count (to get you
into the best spots). What is interesting is the definition of
the different forms of the word "disable." The broad
medical definition of the word as an adjective has to do
with being physically and mentally impaired. They have
stolen my rectum and driven me into a state of wild and
angry despair. But this does not count.

If you look at the word, as a verb, in the sense of "to
disable someone" then we are talking about injuring an
animal in a way that takes away that animal's ability to
perform one or more natural activities. I can still perform
all of my natural activities, but only in an unnatural way.
Regardless, I know that they would not give me
handicapped license plates, and so I have not asked for
them, and I do not drive a car. I drive a small motorcycle,
and I park it fuck-all everywhere and anywhere I want.

I most enjoy to drive it, in its lowest gear, past the motion
sensing doors of supermarkets and other similar stores,
and then park as close as I can to the registers. You might
think that this would cause a commotion, and that people
would try to stop me. But there is an inherent evolutionary
wisdom that runs just below the consciousness of most
people. It is this silent wisdom that tells people, that if

what they just saw happen, actually happened, it is perhaps best not to trouble or probe the issue - that at that moment it is best to stand back and let things play out. They are correct in this. It is wisest to leave my motorcycle alone, by the registers, while I fetch some tonic water and a few things in the produce aisle.

THIRTY ONE

The first photos of Cancertalkerous Melonomames were captured on a video camera system in the subway. The images capture Cancertalkerous pushing an old man onto the tracks, just as the train is pulling into the station. There was no time for anyone to even step forward before the train hit the old man. They are dark and awful photos it is better not to see. And they cannot be unseen, though they must be studied, as they show us glimpses of that which we are hunting. I examined the still photos the department had sent over to my house, and then posted them on the diagram behind the fish tank, so that Ampoule could study them as well.

Melonomames was a tall, lean, and muscular white man, who was completely bald. Perhaps most noticeably he had a perfect tan. He had a deep, rich, perfectly uniform tan. The best tan I had ever seen. The best tan the world had ever seen. After all, he had nothing to fear, I supposed, from the sun.

There was something strange about the photos. There was a boy standing next to Melonomames who seemed to be unfazed by the proceedings around him. He did not react to the man being thrown in front of the train, and he stood next to Melonomames with a surprising physical closeness. His body was positioned in a manner that was open to Melonomames. There was something strange about it. The fish and I stared and stared at it. There was something about it.

They knew each other.

It was Cancertalkerous Melonomames's son. One of his children had survived.

THIRTY TWO

What a wonder is a pomegranate. To cut one cleanly open and then pick at the seeds, which come apart in more ragged and ragged clumps, as you go. The seeds, oh the seeds have a red ethereal light to them. They are neither sweet nor not sweet, and they crunch with herbivorous satisfaction when you eat them. Cold and wet, the individual seeds are woven next to each other in a honeycomb like fashion that is beautiful to behold. Each one stands out so distinctly. Each a perfectly contained red rhombic dodecahedron against the bright yellowish white background that is the pulp. It is a high pleasure to greedily pluck off the individual seeds and eat them rapidly. Crushing them without thinking about them - while thinking about them - all the same. As I eat the pomegranate piece by piece, seed by seed, I think of the gang I am chasing down and taking apart, piece by piece, man by man. I place each one in my mouth and crush it. Knowing that there is now one less to be crushed. I shall crush them all. I shall pick through this fruit, this pomegranate, and consume it all. It is a good fruit to hold in the hand. It sustains.

~

I stopped at a playground on the way home and sat on a bench at the edge of the park. A young, attractive woman sat on another bench at the far end of the park. Two young girls ran around in the contained sand. Running from the swings to the jungle gym, then to the slides and back again. They seemed to get along very well, and they laughed and squealed as they went. Their high voices carried in the air over to me. I stayed until they left, and then left myself, making the final leg of the journey home.

The grass on the front lawn had grown longer than I remembered it. It was now almost a foot tall. I had missed, somehow, the transformation of the grass from being very short and young to being significantly older and taller. Some would say I should cut it, the grass, but I do not abide by some. I have read that it is only when the grass reaches a significant height of a foot or more that it may actually reproduce naturally. It is not for me to stop it.

I went into the house, prepared some herbal tea with tequila and honey, smoked some marijuana, took a large number of pills, and then headed down to the basement to practice shooting, to await the onset of exhaustion.

THIRTY THREE

My father has always urged me towards visibility when it comes to matters of the road, and he has been correct in this. It is remarkable how many men slink around on jet-black motorcycles, in jet-black gear, praying, it seems, that no one will see them. We do not move in this fashion, as we have undertaken the love of the sun. We ride proud and tall, albeit slowly and in a smaller space, we raise the banner of the sun. We are yellow. There is no flag that may fly higher. Lest we forget, the ratio of the earth to the sun is one million to one. We ride with the sun.

I stopped to visit my father, when I was out on errands. He is very old and likes to tell me things that I have heard before. Things that I have heard, although sometimes, to be fair, I have not really heard them. Sometimes I am unable to hear. He talked to me about the stars. He told me how the components that made up former stars, which had long ago imploded, were interwoven in all matter, in all places and all time. The higher elements on the Periodic Table were not of this world. They were of stars.

"We are all of us," he said, "made of stars. We are both beneath and of them."

It is something to think about. We spoke for a while. The day grew on towards night for us both, and then we said our goodbyes and I made my way home, while he remained there, quiet and still, within his home.

We are all fallen stars.

THIRTY FOUR

Every time my motorcycle breaks down, I know that I must fix it, but it is never clear to me that I will be able to, until I have, in fact, fixed it. Of course, I must fix it. And so I do.

I stopped, one morning, at The Architect's on my way to the hospital. He is an architect of the internet, and works to create and shape areas of it. I am always teasing him and cajoling him to hide code on the internet. Little things that people could find and discover. As people need more surprises. More mystery. Strange links and pieces of information. Humor. We could always use more humor.

He was in his garage preparing his bike for a ride. The Architect had a beautiful motorcycle. One of the prettiest I have seen. It had been a gift from his family. One of the perks of staying alive. Melonomames had attacked The Architect too. He had injured his head. One of the worst injuries you can have. But he was a tough bastard and he had gotten through it. He was clean now. He still had to do scans all the time, but, Hell, who didn't?

The Architect put down the rag he'd been using on the bike, stood up and shook my hand. "It's good to see you, Hors. I'm sorry to have heard," he said.

I touched my side without meaning to, and said, "I'm in with Chemagi, The Turtle, Irinotecan and The Knights. Cancertalkerous is fucked. He doesn't stand a chance." We both smiled and then headed upstairs for a shot of bourbon. It was good to see The Architect, but I couldn't stay for long. It was good to talk to him, as he understands things that others can only imagine, as he has been marked as I. But the days are short. We said all the things we had to say, and I soon got back on my way towards the hospital.

We did not speak of it that day, but The Architect's mother had been killed by Cancertalkerous's men several years before. Too many mothers had died. We were going to try and stop it. We were going to try and stop Him. We were going to try and change things. There had already been too much sorrow.

THIRTY FIVE

Irinotecan was a handsome man and he spent the majority of my therapy sessions (though he was assigned to protect me) over at the nurses' station - chatting up the single female nurses. I couldn't blame him. I would have joined him, but I had sworn my allegiance to another long ago. Though she does not appear directly in this story, I must respect her, even in my fiction. As the worlds of fact and fiction are tied more closely than you think, and one must tread carefully among magic and prophesy. It is always good advice to uphold your true beliefs and loves always, whether you travel to the deepest levels of fantasy, sorrow, ecstasy, boredom, danger, despair, anger, or ennui. Keep always with you what you need to keep with you, in order to keep being you. Do not ask anyone else what this is to be. It is a question that you alone may know the answer to. But rest assured that it is an answer that you may always find. You know more than you know. And you will all do well. Whether or not I can be with you at every step of the process, you will do well. With just a tiny bit of luck, you will live long and be prosperous, as I am sending you all that I can right now, through the power of these pages. Stories and ideas have more power than some know. They are what pull us through the darkest moments of the night, and have the power to call the morning sun back round again - back again, each day, to show us the way through - whether the day be cloudy or bright. The sun shines behind clouds - always. You might not fully know it yet, but you already have all that you need. Trust yourself.

But I have gotten off topic. Rinno liked to chat up the nurses at their station, and they didn't seem to mind his company. Sometimes, though, he was called back into the immediacy of the moment. As happened late one night towards the end of my therapy.

I was walking out of my hospital room to go to the bathroom, when an orderly I didn't recognize bumped into my IV stand and knocked it over. He apologized profusely, and then took several moments to go about righting it. When the bags and cables were all settled, he apologized again, looked at his pager and then excused himself, quickly, as he was needed on another floor. I resumed shuffling down the hall, pulling the IV stand along with me, singing a little under my breath as I walked.

When I reached the bathroom door, the orderly was disappearing around a corner, smiling and waving as he went. The bathroom was unoccupied, so I pushed the large wooden door open, slid the IV stand into the room and then let the door close behind me. Bathrooms are never the best places in chemotherapy wards. Everyone who uses them, all of the patients anyway, are tweaked and on average there tends to be more urine on things than you generally find in other bathrooms. In addition, there are plastic chamber pots, with tissues over them, waiting in the corner to be emptied. The pots are from those who are too far gone to go in any other fashion. But you make the best of it.

I used the edge of my shoe to carefully raise the lid of the toilet seat, and was preparing to go about my business, when the alarm on my IV stand went off, and I realized that I was out of the drug that was being administered. Or at least there was a blockage. I pulled the IV stand close to me so that I could inspect it. Everything up top looked good, the bag was still about 1/3 full and none of the tubing was kinked or blocked. The drip was still dripping. Nothing seemed to be occluded. There was no reason for the IV alarm to be going off. I looked down at the controls, and everything seemed fine - there were no warnings or error codes. But the alarm still continued to go off. Then I looked down, all the way, to the wire basket at the base of the IV stand, and that was when I saw the bomb. It had a large digital timer on the side of it, with extravagant wires, and it was now emitting a loud buzzing sound, as it counted down the final seconds to detonation - clearly they had created it with the intention that it would elicit my attention only at the very end (at my very end) to ensure that I, personally, would be aware of my final predicament, yet be unable to do anything about it. (Cancertalkerous Melonomames was, after all, a very sick and clever man.) According to the timer on the side of the bomb, we were now down to seven seconds. That was what we had left.

I immediately called out to my partner through the closed door, "Rinno! We've got C-4 in here! Get everyone out!"

Irinotecan kicked open the heavy wooden door and ran in. He scoped the room, saw the explosives, grabbed onto my torso with his hands, and kicked the entire IV Stand out of the bathroom with tremendous force. The needles and patches and cables that had been attached to my body flew off as the IV stand hurtled out of the room - into an open supply closet, across the hall, where if fell over. Rinno then slammed the door closed and threw us both to the ground. The bomb exploded in the storage room and some of the walls around us caught fire. Automated sprinkler systems kicked in, and orderlies, agents, officers, and nurses came running with fire extinguishers. The fires were relatively quickly contained but it took a long time for the noise to die down. Everything was wet, disheveled and charred.

Word eventually got to us that the hospital staff had caught the foot soldier (who'd been disguised as an orderly) and they had him handcuffed down in the hallway in the basement, by the grief room. Irinotecan and I took the elevator down in silence.

In fact, it turned out that he wasn't *disguised* as an orderly. He *was* an orderly. He had been with us, on our side of the light. He had been on our team. He had been helping and they had *gotten* to him. They had turned him. They had spread. It had happened so quickly, no one had been able to realize it or stop it. That was how the malignancy spread. It spread subtly. It spread quickly. No one was safe. No one was immune.

The walls in the hospital's basement were dull white and poorly lit, and there were three men standing at the end of the hall. The orderly's hands were handcuffed behind his back, and there was a guard on either side of him. Irinotecan and I reached the end of the corridor. We were now all standing just outside the grieving room, which was empty. Handsfull stepped out from the supply room next to us, and stood silently, watching the captive. He had never really gotten over the absence of his golden. His retriever that had been killed by Lymphatico.

95

Rinno never liked to carry a regular gun. He preferred to carry a stun gun, and a long knife, both in clips on his belt. He unsheathed his knife and approached the handcuffed man, and sidled up very close to him. He smelled him and asked, "You planted the bomb?" The gang member looked at him defiantly and said, "Yeah, I planted the bomb," and then he started to say something else, but Irinotecan interrupted him by sinking the knife into his heart. Then he jiggled it and he simply held it there. And finally, Rinno spoke. He spoke directly into the cancer at the core of the man, and said, "You will cause no more grief, now, forever."

Irinotecan then turned to Handsfull, and said to him, "Nothing *golden* shall be hurt again." (It hadn't actually been Lymphatico that he had killed, it was a low-level henchman, but it was a good line and we all appreciated it.) Handsfull nodded, returned to his supply room, and closed the door.

And that was that. We put the remains in a heavy duty bio-waste bag, by the dumpsters. Irinotecan tagged the bag with the sign of Melonomames's gang, crushed ovals piled randomly on top of one another, allowing them to come and retrieve it, to do with it what they would. Then we headed back up to the chemotherapy ward to check on security and to see who had been injured. To find out what had been damaged. To see what we could do to help. To settle in and work through the rest of the night to try and fix that which had been broken. To try and restore.

THIRTY SIX

There is magic in carbonation. I love the effervescence of carbonated water - the static crackle of the bubbles and the slight discomfort involved with drinking it quickly - the beginnings of involuntary tears in the corner of the eyes - potential tears that are quickly reabsorbed. I rarely drink un-carbonated water, as I find no satisfaction in it. It is only carbonation for me. And then there is the strange business of the creature that is Carbon Dioxide. Deadly in the air, at high concentrations, yet safe and delicious when infused into a liquid. I imagine sometimes that it is, in fact, still deadly in liquid, though they simply haven't figured it out yet. Sometimes, discoveries of this nature take hundreds of years. It was not too long ago that people ate off of leaden plates, mercury thermometers have only just left us, and they still struggle to carefully dig asbestos out of buildings.

It does not matter to me, though, if my carbonated water is, in fact, harmful, as it brings me creature comfort and satisfaction in the here and now. I shall stick with it regardless.

~

To be chronically ill is, to be honest, (on some levels) a gift. It heightens your senses. It increases your ability to discern elements of the universe around you. In fact, the adjustment to the senses, from being chronically ill, is so significant that it gives the sick a small but clear and discernible advantage over the healthy. And the healthy, for the most part, don't even realize this. I see things that the healthy do not see. I understand things that the healthy do not understand (as many of my chronically ill brethren do). We have a heightened sense of reality that allows us to act with a vastly magnified impact, within vastly narrowed corridors of time. We get things done.

Do not get me wrong, the healthy are there with us, in the corridor, but they are not as aware of the confines around them. They are walking. They are walking along, ambling, stopping to pause and fuss with things of minor import - minor problems - while we are running past them (carrying enormous burdens), at remarkable, remarkable speeds.

Note, though, that this speed is only frantic in terms of cognition. In terms of physical movement, we sometimes barely move at all. In fact, some of us have stopped moving all together.

But what you do not realize is that the chronically injured boy, slumped over in the corner, in the wheelchair - that physically frozen boy - is, in fact, moving. Moving, moving, moving. Unseen fingers, nimbly, nimbly, nimbly, fiddling with the wires and transistors that you cannot see - (the capacitors) woven into the very fabric of the bomb that has been placed in his lap. He is defusing it - right there - right now - though you may not see his fingers move. We are defusing the bombs to help prevent devastation to all of those in the corridor with us, sometimes at great risk to ourselves, but we are often successful and it is worth it. Though you may not have realized any of this - it does not mean that it is not occurring right in front of you. We, the chronically ill, are busy.

We have powers.

And the powers have us. So be it.

~

And what of when we feel darkness? When it sneaks into our hearts? It is okay, to let it into your heart a little. Let it in, let it see the beauty and then ban it from there. Show it the joy it may not experience and send it from there (away).

We regroup. We pick ourselves up off the ground. Here's how you do it:

Wait for the motorcycle to stop sliding. When it has, turn off the engine, stand up and lift the bike up beneath you. Look down across yourself and the machine, very briefly, to ensure to that all essential systems are still functioning - then turn the bike back on - assess traffic and drive down the road - to a parking lot. Get off the bike and assess the windshield, chain and tires. If the foot pegs, which are immobile - have been bent out of position - leverage the pegs back (to within a reasonable tolerance of their starting positions) with your feet and legs. Check the oil and the reserve pistol, in the storage compartment. Get back on the motorcycle - in your full gear (combat boots, over-pants, leather gloves, reinforced jacket, and full face helmet) and then tear out of the parking lot.

You must do this, too, when darkness intrudes. Do not

fear it. Welcome it in. You have known it was coming. Prepare it a cup of tea. As it looks like it could quite use a good cup of tea.

There are some things that you must engage and spin round the room with, almost as though in a dance. This is one of those things. Engage it. Bravery is only fear acted through.

THIRTY SEVEN

When it rains, the leather of the gloves stains my hands black. It sinks in, pressed by the wind, and when I arrive, soaked through, at my destination, the gloves are wet and thick, and they peel off like an extra layer of skin. My hands emerge dark. Dark-red and black - stiff from having gripped the handlebars fiercely, and they are blackened (from the ink) - stained for the rest of the day.

But it is only through discomfort that we may ever appreciate comfort. It is only through sadness that we know joy. Coldness - warmth.

Though it is often raw out - it is always interesting. There is always something there worth looking at, despite the cold and the wetness. It is always worth trying and fighting. Despite the ice-cream headaches. Despite the pain. I am often the only motorcyclist I see out, on days when it is worst. I look for my brethren, on those days, but almost invariably I find that they have not come out with me to play.

Of course, the road conditions on those days are terrible. They are dangerous and deadly - simple mistakes, of no particular consequence on any other day, can kill you outright. But the conditions are real. The conditions may occur to any motorcyclist at any time. They may hamper you. You may be hampered. Prepare, with me, to be hampered. Drive with me - slowly and determinedly in the rain. There are times in your life when you may need to, for whatever reason, jump onto a small motorcycle in the driving rain, and then *make it* to a certain destination at a certain time. Or else it will all fall apart.

And so, we train in the rain. We train in the rain, and I welcome it. The hammer of my 19-shot semi-automatic BB pistol is cocked and ready - a short reach from either hand. Do not forget - we have been fucked with, and we are returning now - with a wrath of the ages - with the wrath of the sun. We are pillaging the predators. We travel with the light of the sun. That which was sodden and sad, that which was bloated and nearly drowned, shall be dried out and made whole again, with the breath of the wind: the wind that circles wildly around us.

What you don't, perhaps, know yet, is that we have already broken the rules of the game and of chance. We were not supposed to get this far, and yet we have. We are a hardened object. A projectile sprung from a powerful bow. We are arching up in the air, and we shall come down, ever so shortly, on our opponent, piercing down with a sharpened fishhook-like end. We shall break through malignancy - a sharpened spear hewn from the olive tree. The truces are over. We ride forth, as we sing.

We are a force, that at first glance, appears to be incredibly un-forceful. To look at us, there does not appear to be too much to be reckoned with. And perhaps, on some level, that is the truth. Yet there may be something there. Perhaps it is best to let it pass, almost unnoticed.

But I have gotten off track.

The Teacher lived far north of the city. She was wild and lived off the land, hunting and growing things as needed. She could tell you about when they intentionally flooded a small rural town near to her, when they cut down all the trees and then burned them, before they buried the town with water from The Dead River. She could tell you this and more. The children listened to her because she was wild and direct, and because she wouldn't cut down their trees and burn them.

I called her on my way home, but missed her, as she was out.

THIRTY EIGHT

There is a silhouetted woman in repose on the trim of my motorcycle, by the wheel well. She has tiny embedded light emitting diodes and is wired into the low-beam setting of the headlight. Whenever the motorcycle is running, with the headlight on low, she glows. As we need all the light in this world that we may find.

The windshield is split, or almost fully split, in half. There is a large crack that runs three-quarters of the way across the shield. I have addressed it with clear duct tape that covers the high strength clear epoxy, which I used to fill the actual gap. The windshield and I have been through many scrapes together. There are two metallic stickers on the windshield: on the right side an angel, on the left side a devil: my two muses with whom I ride, as I try to stay balanced between them. The devil and the angel are both extremely fit women, shown in silhouette. Some may object to this, and they may be correct to do so, but I would posit that if you must stare into the gates of heaven and hell for a prolonged period of time, it is best to enjoy the view. It is best to make sure that there is something in it that will make you smile. We must not forget to enjoy a little bit of absurdity and outrageousness.

The motorcycle and I have certain similarities. We are both prematurely-old and delicate. Such is the bond I share with my bike. Cheaply made and somewhat prone to disaster, it is difficult, at best, to find even the simplest of parts for either one of us. And so we make a point of trying not to break things.

And when things do break, as they must, when things do break, we fix them the best we can. And when we must, we learn to live with the truly broken parts that may not be made whole again.

THIRTY NINE

So, I don't drive a car. I ride my motorcycle, or I walk.

It is funny because every time I get on my motorcycle, I am relatively certain that I am going to die.

It is funny because every time I walk through the front door of the hospital, I am relatively certain that I am going to die.

Though I have not. I have not died, I have survived to fight another day, and I will continue to do so, until this is over. I am hunting sickness and malignancy itself. I am the light chasing the darkness. I am the sun that is poised to rise over the ridge. The Boognish from the outer realm.

I will tell you right now, in the middle of all this, the secret of everything, although I probably shouldn't, and they will likely make my time shorter for having done so. The secret of everything is as follows: life, the universe, and everything is the *process* of light overcoming darkness. It is a continual process without end. Darkness does not prevail, lightness does not prevail. It is a continual process in which light is always slightly overcoming dark. One in which both must always be present. The system would not be able to sustain itself in any other fashion.

Your relation to the God-Head is one in which a metal colander has been placed over a fantastic light source. You are one of the circles of light, a point of light on the side of the colander, which is tied directly back to the fantastic light source. You are part and parcel of the light source, whether you are aware of it or not.

You are the fantastic light source.

Now you know. Back to the story.

FORTY

It is the fall now.

This story takes place over days. It takes place over months and years, but, the entire story really all takes place in the fall. In the fall and in its transition to winter. That is where it resides. That is where it is.

The spring, the summer, and the winter, all have their place. This I will not deny. They all have their place, and I enjoy them all, as is reasonable.

But there is something electric, in the fall, which is not present in other seasons. Bright, sharp days made up cleanly of light and shadow: neither hot nor cold, with winds that cut precisely through everything. A poignant poignancy.

It is in the fall that we reside.

~

In the morning, I ate a bowl of hempen granola with water, as there was no milk. (It is, anyway, a good idea to eat your cereal, every now and then, with water instead of milk, as it is only then that you get a true sense of what you are really eating.) I also drank half a bottle of tonic water with quinine, and then headed out. The cane, at my side, filled with a dark tropical rum.

I enjoy the bitter taste of quinine, as *it*, the bitterness, is a taste that has largely evaporated from the palate of the

Western world. Although it shouldn't have. If you do not thoroughly know and understand bitter, you cannot fully appreciate sweet.

FORTY ONE

Sometimes I feel that no matter where I am, no matter what I am doing, I am, in some way, heading towards the hospital.

~

It is funny, perhaps, but I never feel more alone than in the middle of a large group. My hearing has not been very good, for a while now. And I have always had a hard time, with names and faces. There are times when everyone around me is talking to someone else, and the collective din of the bar rises to a strange point where it becomes almost perfectly quiet. At those times, I look above the crowd, to the televisions above which I cannot hear, and all I can think about, all I can see, in those moments, are the gang members I am still chasing down and fighting.

I am going to kill them all.

Just for that alone. Just for making me think of the malignancy. For drawing my thoughts away from the party, for drawing me from the gathering, from the warmth of the collective fire.

I will kill them all for that alone.

FORTY TWO

I ate lunch by myself at a picnic table in one of the parks I visit. I was halfway through eating slices I had cut from a slab of semi-hard Tomme. I had put the slices on crackers designed to wonderfully mimic small pieces of toast, rows of which I had carefully arranged on the plate in front of me. I had counted them out and kept the edges lined up nicely. They were quite good - they crunched forcibly when you bit them - and I washed them down with an old tawny port which enlivened my senses and rounded everything out. There is a bottomless richness to a good tawny port. It rings round in the mouth and sings.

Lymphatico emerged then from the trees at the edge of the park. He walked slowly over to my table, with a large caliber handgun drawn and pointed at my chest the entire time. I nodded to him, when he reached my table, and asked him to join me, though we did not shake hands. He sat directly across from me - the gun still pointed at me, though he placed his arm on its side and rested it on the table - I believe to lower his profile and lessen the risk of drawing attention from passersby.

I had wondered where and when he would find me, and how I would feel about it when he did. I was down to a final sip of port, by the time Lymphatico settled across from me. I lifted my glass to my adversary and drank what was left. I did not hold the liquid in my mouth, but simply drank it down, as true savoring is not done in the mouth, but in the brain.

He started to speak. He said, "I have come to kill you, esse."* He then started to say something else, but I interrupted him.

"Do you really know why I am fighting you?" I asked. I shall tell you, now, before we end this. Sit and listen to the lesson, before it is gone from you. I am okay with dying as a grown man. I have already made it to forty-one years old. I have survived well into full adulthood. Many of the greatest achievements of human kind were completed, both in current times and long before, by men and women who died well before the age of forty-one. I have had plenty of time. That is not the issue. The problem is that it is *almost always* bad form to die on young children."

I had been saying all of this directly into Lymphatico's eyes, and while his eyes did not stray from mine, I could see that he was becoming more and more antsy as I continued.

"Shut the fuck up, Man!" he shouted.

*It had initially startled me that Lymphatico had used the slang *esse* to refer to me, as the term is usually used primarily among gangs, solely to address other members. I was clearly not a member of his gang. In fact, I was diametrically opposed to him and all that he represented. But the more I thought about it, the more I realized that although we were in direct conflict (on the surface) we were also inexorably tied together, somehow, in ways that could not necessarily be separated or pulled apart. We were the two sides of the coin.

I continued, "And so, you see, I am obligated to do everything in my power to avoid that from happening. I will do anything to try and ensure that I may spend at least a few more years with my girls to help show them the basic structures and organizations of the world, and to help show them how they must navigate them. Many of these lessons are complex and nuanced and cannot properly be taught and transferred at a young age."

Lymphatico jolted his gun up from the table, raised it to my head, and screamed, "I told you to shut the fuck up!"

I am not terribly familiar with real hand guns, but it appeared that Lymphatico was pointing a gorgeously maintained, silver .44 caliber handgun at my face, and what really made it miraculous, what really made the whole thing exciting, was that there was a fantastic engraving on the side of the barrel. Someone had taken the time and the care - the love - to engrave the image of a spectral wraith, reaching out along the barrel of the gun, towards the muzzle. It was expertly done, and I could not help but admire it.

"The cheese, by the way, is quite good," I said. I gestured down towards the plate. "It's a semi-hard Tomme, but I don't know if you're into that."

"Silencio!" Lymphatico roared.

"And so I will. I will be quiet, in time," I said. "But first, a final riddle. What did the .177 caliber steel BBs say to The Enormous Dickhead? They said, 'Bang, bang, bang, bang, bang, bang, bang, bang!'" And with that I fired 19 shots into Lymphatico's groin from under the table. I had caught him slightly by surprise, and while he was able to pull the trigger on his own gun, the initial impacts of the BBs passing through his penis and scrotum had thrown him off enough that his hand had moved slightly to the side, and the bullet from his gun flew safely past my head.

Lymphatico dropped his gun and leaned forward, reaching tenderly down to his groin to try and gauge what had just happened. As he leaned forward, I picked up the cheese knife from off of the table and stabbed it into his right lung, wiggled it, and then stabbed into his left, where I left it. This got his attention and caused him to reel back and look at me.

"You are the kind of person who places forks and knives pointing upwards in the dishwasher," I said. "Their sharpened tines and blades reaching out to try and cut me," I continued. "You wish for them to cut me, as I reach past, and yet I avoid them. I avoid your trap. Do you pretend, *to yourself*, that the handles of the upward facing utensils will not slide through the holes in the bottom of the silverware basket? That they will not block the rotor of the very machine itself? Do you *honestly* think that they will not jam the sliding capability of the entire lower shelf-tray?"

Do you not see the results of your own actions?"

I paused and then added, "Do you realize that you have done things which may *never* be forgiven?"

And with that, I stopped looking into Lymphatico's eyes. I gave him a slight push and he fell over backwards onto the ground behind the bench. I placed a call to the department to have them come and process the scene, and then I packed up the remains of my lunch and headed home.

I had thought that I would feel tired but satisfied. That I would have been flushed and proud, but in the end, I felt primarily tired and sick.

Though I was, in all honesty, a little bit proud, and I could not, despite myself, stop grinning.

FORTY THREE

The funny thing about evading death, is that after you do it, you cannot help but be conscious of the fact that death shall at some point try again. That it will return for you.

You must be aware of this and come to terms with it.

But, for all of the darkness and violence of this story, do not be misguided, it is, in fact, (at its heart), a story of hope and love. There will always be sickness and ill-health. They shall always exist. They shall not go away. Nor would I have them do so, when we really get down to it. There will always be sadness and sickness, but they are tied intrinsically to well being and laughter. You cannot have one without the other. All we can ask is to try and make a good go of it - to enjoy it, as it unfolds. I have enjoyed it. I have no complaints, and only a few regrets. I hope that you may enjoy the experiences that unfold before you, and I hope that this note finds you well.

FORTY FOUR

There are stars on the ceiling of my bedroom. They are old sticker-stars. They were put up by a previous owner, many years ago, and were painted over long before I got to them, and they have been painted over again, since.

They no longer shine.

In fact, they are hard to make out. You must look closely for them. They appear only as slightly raised surfaces - they are the same color as the background. White on white. But they are stars all the same.* And they warm my heart, when it needs warming, as it often does, and they remind me of the larger sense of play, which I am often in danger of forgetting.

And I love them.

I crawled into my bed, in my pajamas, after eating and drinking what I could. I got under the thick, brightly colored comforter that is covered with mystical designs and let the satisfying weight of the bedding rest on my legs. Warm and soft light from the lamp on my nightstand shone down upon me.

*Former sources of light, their light is no longer being generated, but still it travels across time towards you. It is there to be seen, should you choose to look for it.

PomPom The Cat came and sat with me. PomPom sat on my lap and I petted her. I scratched beneath her chin and she rolled onto her side and curled up into a ball, although she is no longer a kitten. I continued to scratch and pet her, as I sat and thought. She purred almost inaudibly. I ate a variety of pills from my nightstand and washed them down with a good whiskey, then both she and I fell fast asleep.

PomPom is a polydactyl Maine coon, and she has two extra toes on each of her front paws. (What a joy are extra cat toes!) She is gentle and affectionate with people but has a complex dichotomy in which she is also a highly effective and vicious hunter of birds and small woodland creatures. It is not uncommon for me to find fully decapitated chipmunks in the driveway, though she has never scratched a person. She has never scratched an adult, or a child, no matter how roughly they have treated her.

In addition, she does not jump up on the tables or counters around the house, though she is fully capable of doing so - as I have seen her jump over the six-foot fence in the backyard with ease. She chooses not to jump on things around the house, as she is well mannered and thoughtful.

And I love her.

FORTY FIVE

When I was young, I would get up early on schooldays and sit with my mother to have breakfast with her before she left for work. She actually worked for the hospital then. For years and years, she worked at the hospital, but no one we knew (then) was sick and fighting. Not back then.

We sat on small wicker chairs, by the radiator, by the front window. After eating, she would drink her tea and look out the window, and I would curl up on the couch, underneath the blanket - making a game of seeing how tightly I could compress myself - how close around me I could pull the blanket: drifting in and out of sleep, until it was time for my mother to leave. Then I headed upstairs to watch television. The machines did not run through the night then, as they do now. The stations did not broadcast in the darkness. I waited, each morning, for the testing pattern on the television to turn into the national anthem, then I watched the first two programs of the day (whatever they happened to be showing in that particular time slot) before it was time for me to leave and walk to school.

School was a sad and awkward experience, that I never, in all my years, learned to master. So it goes. So it went.

~

My mother called me when I was returning home from the hospital, on the train, on a particularly gray and rainy afternoon. I don't know what we said, but we spoke the truth, as we always do with one another, and we laughed and laughed about life and death. We just talked and laughed, and it was nice, in a special way. It was nice to be able to laugh with my mother about life and death.

I initially had the words here, that she and I said, but then I removed them. (And, now, I no longer recall them.)

You don't, in the end, need to know everything, after all.

FORTY SIX

Marijuana is a tricky creature. Cancer therapies have come a long way and the anti-nausea drugs that are prescribed now by hospitals are often effective enough to stop you from being truly nauseous. They are clever and well designed to the point that vomiting is a very rare process, and may, in fact, be entirely absent from an entire (chemotherapy) regimen, which could last for months. The hospital drugs are good, and they may stop you from throwing up, but they can't actually stop you from feeling awful and worn down. And this is where marijuana comes in. Marijuana can bring a lightness and a levity to the most worn down of situations. It can reintroduce humor and hunger into situations where it has long been absent. But, as I have said, it can also be tricky. There is a very delicate balance of getting it just right. A small amount can lighten the room significantly, but it is very easy to have too much, and to lose too much of oneself. Sometimes it can be something as small and simple as having two hits, instead of one. It can sneak up on you and destroy your short term memory, putting anxiety and an inability to accurately read social cues (including your own) in its place. It can destroy your ability to converse properly with those around you -as much and as strongly - as being severely drunk. To the point that, sometimes, your only recourse (if you're smart) is to sit quietly in the corner of the room and wait for it to pass. And it will pass. This is what I have found. A little bit is sublime, but a little bit more is sublimely difficult, and it is hard to get it right.

I must speak briefly on heroin. You must understand, dear reader, that it is one of the things in this universe that is almost certain to eventually destroy you, after only a single exposure. There may be a delay before its awfulness plays fully out, but that does not mean it is not coming.

There are simply some things that may not be dabbled in. Heroin is one of them.

There is no room for error in this.

FORTY SEVEN

I can't get the poison off of my teeth.

That is the thought that occurs to you, when you realize that you cannot get the poison off of your teeth. It comes with months of chemotherapy. All of the drugs you're constantly taking. I cannot get the coating of chemicals off of my teeth. It is something that is there, but it isn't. It's on your teeth, but it isn't, and it won't go away. You can't brush or rinse it away. It's in them. It is there, the poison on your teeth, and the taste in the back of your mouth.

Off. It tastes *off*. As you yourself, when you taste it, are *off*.

But this is what you must do. You must charge yourself up. You must prepare yourself for battle. If you live long enough, you will go to battle, everyone who lives long enough eventually does.

I am at battle right now.

I don't even mind it on some levels. Someone must battle. Better myself than some other person. Certainly not the children. There is nothing worse than sickness in children. There is nothing harder. There is no well of sadness deeper. But I am not there, I am not dealing with that, and for that, I am thankful.

FORTY EIGHT

I returned home late and took the back approach. I passed quietly through the parking lot of the apartment complex, situated directly behind my house. I passed in shadow. Keeping my presence unknown to any around me. As I neared the fence that borders the two properties, I spotted two gang members hidden between some dumpsters.

They must have been sent to check on me. But it was very late. I was returning far later than they had expected. They had given up on me, it appeared. The gang members were young: a man and a woman. They both had the same black leather jackets that all of Melonomames's crew wore, with red armbands and the haphazardly stacked ovals, but the woman was topless, except for her coat, while the man had his pants partway off. Both gang members looked to be in very good physical shape, and I thought to myself, "Why are they working for him? What had gone wrong inside them?"

The two did not notice me. They were deeply engaged in what they were doing, whispering words to each other that I could not hear.

I got very, very close to them, without them realizing, and then I stepped out calmly from behind the dumpsters and said, "Hey there, neighbors, could I borrow a stick of butter?" Then I looked down at the man's crotch, and said, "Oh, hey, never mind, it looks like you're down to a quarter stick, I'll just use some olive oil instead. Thanks."

And I smiled warmly at them.

And with that, of course, I pulled out my BB pistol and began firing. They ran, pulling themselves together the best they could, as they headed down the steep embankment of the ravine, stumbling towards the stream at the bottom, in the darkness.

I couldn't do it. The first ten shots went way over their heads. I should have just pointed my gun directly into the air, as though it were a starter pistol. I guess, on some level, it was. They had been readying themselves, at the starting line, though they didn't know it, and when the gun went off, they dutifully took off running.

I fired over them, but as the man was just about to disappear from my view, as he was just about to pass beyond my range, I shot him squarely three times in the ass. And I could see that the BBs found their target, as he reached back, wildly, while he was running, though he did not stop. The BBs in his ass would only go in about half-an-inch at that range. They would be able to dig them out with only moderate difficulty.

It would give them something to do.

Who knows, maybe the interruption would be enough to allow them to break free from the gang, so that they could find their own way. I liked to think so.

In the end, I chose not to shoot the woman at all. Perhaps that is sexist of me. I am thinking now, that I probably should have shot the woman, as that would be the only fair thing do. But she had had nice breasts and it seemed a strange thing to shoot such a creature. But it was not fair, and I probably should have shot her.

I decided that I would probably shoot her next time, should we meet again.

My house was being watched, albeit poorly, at times. It was being watched all the same.

FORTY NINE - PUSSY PERIL

When you have cancer for a prolonged period of time, when it keeps coming back, as it often does, the hospital tries to make certain amenities for you. They try to assign you the same chemotherapy nurse, so that, as you return, over months and years, there will be some continuity. I was assigned a very good nurse. She was funny and kind, but straightforward and she could thread a needle through your arm like a seamstress.

She was caring and considerate, but she was tough and reserved, as well. I usually carried on wildly, waving my arms around and singing, in the mornings, making a scene (at the beginning of my sessions) but one can only fight so much, and as the relentless therapy drugs sank in, as the treatments went on, towards the afternoons, I would eventually grow quiet and reserved. She would always notice this and comment on it directly. She would say something to the effect of, "You're not acting up so much anymore now, are you?" And I would acquiesce and nod my head. She was right. The drugs were strong. Stronger than you may realize. The drugs affected patients so strongly, *so strongly*, that they (the patients) could be wickedly thrown by even the simplest unconscious associations with them. My nurse would confide to me that she had some patients who vomited upon seeing her, so great was the association with their nausea.

I, personally, whenever I saw her, always congratulated her - that she did not yet make me vomit.

Let me be clear, though, she was excellent. She was funny and kind, and I always liked her. I often thought, as she treated me, 'So many of her patients must die. I wonder if I am one of her patients who will die?' That is something I often thought about, when I looked at her, as we spoke.

~

Irinotecan ran into the chemo infusion ward late one morning and burst into the room where I was being treated. Brigid, my chemotherapy nurse, was applying an IV to my arm when Rinno shouted out, "Come on! We've got to go. They've stolen a litter of kittens and they're going to kill them!"

"Shit!" I shouted. "I'm sorry, Brigid, we've got to go!" I pulled all of the medical apparatuses off of my body, pushed the IV stand to the side of the room and jumped up to follow Irinotecan out of the ward.

It was a long day that stretched out into a long night, but in the end we caught the bastard who'd taken the kittens. He had them in a sack on the backseat of his car.

Luckily, he hadn't yet had a chance to do anything with them. The kittens were alright. It was an ugly scene though. I don't quite know what happened but we ended up decapitating him, as he was trying to get out of the car and flee the parking lot. The whole thing required double the normal paper work, and I'm not sure what we said on it, but we got the kittens back safely, and *that*, I think, was what mattered.

There was one thing, though, which was even *more* important.

The most important thing, really, was that I realized then, *that day*, as Irinotecan and I held the kittens, I realized then that no matter what happens, as long as there are people, there shall be kittens. As the two species could simply not live without one another. They simply could not.

I could not.

It was a good and a warm thought and it lifted my spirits thoroughly.

There shall always be kittens.

I know this, now. I know this to be true.

FIFTY

Chance is a funny thing. The chance of something happening, or not happening. We are surrounded by chances. It is interesting to think about.

There are all these unplugged lamps on the small tables set around the waiting room of the infusion ward. They never seem to be plugged in. I don't know why, but no one ever seems to bother to plug them in. Maybe they don't want them plugged in. Many of the lamps aren't even situated near outlets.

When I plug them in, sometimes they come on.

Sometimes, they don't.

I find that I am always greatly encouraged when they do, in fact, come on. What a wonder is light. What a wonderful thing, to see in the darkness, if only for a little ways.

It is very different to see a little, than to see nothing at all.

A simple lamp, in a quiet waiting room, turned on by a simple man. One more source of illumination, one more bright spark by which to see, by which to love, and to fight.

I am always greatly encouraged when the lamps do, in fact, turn on. As this does, sometimes, happen.

FIFTY ONE

There are times when I don't have the energy for the
whole thing. When it doesn't seem worth it. I get tired, and
I like to rest. It feels good to rest: too good. But I push on,
as you push on, not because we must - but because we
choose to. We choose to go on. Periods of darkness and
doubt will pass. (If you let them.) Anger and despair are
but clouds in the sky. They shall disappear quickly - if you
look at them calmly. If you let them. Look at them. See
what they are and then release them. Let them dissipate
into the air before you, as clouds blow apart in the sky.

Still, I ride, and I am armed. As I am hunted. But there is
more to it than that, as I myself am also hunting. We are
on the attack, and we shall not, if we have anything to say
about it, be stopped.

~

I had a simple, pared down lunch: several dozen frozen
tubes of juices. I find the long frozen tubes beautiful: the
rich reds, greens, blues, yellows, oranges, purples and
pinks. Simple sugars and colors added to gorgeous water.
Nothing is more thirst quenching than the slow steady
stream of slushy ice, pushed upwards carefully and
pointedly with thumb and forefinger. My only problem
was that I could not savor them. I devoured one after the
next, as quickly as I could tear off the stiff plastic tops.
(Until they were gone.) Too soon it was time to gather the
empty plastic sleeves and discard them in the trash barrel

near the picnic table. I began to think in analogies of how I would devour the remaining gang members one by one, but lost patience for it, and headed out of the park. There was much to do.

FIFTY TWO

I forgot to tell you about the chemo pump. The pump's timer would count down, for several days, during the portable infusion phase, which began after the initial IV infusion at the hospital, and when it (the pump) got to the end of its cycle it would beep until you dealt with it. An alarm, at the end, every few seconds - an interminable stuck-in-your-head kind of sound. Like a digital timer on an oven. It was like hearing an oven timer going off incessantly at a crowded dinner party. Ringing over the heads of all the guests. I found, at such times, that it was almost impossible to focus on anything else.

That was what it was like, sometimes, in the infusion waiting room.

Patients whose pumps had timed out waited for the nurses to see them - to turn them off. I did not fully understand this, as I myself was shown how to engage and disengage the pump - how to turn it off and pack it up safely in a protective bio-hazard bag (ready for shipping) when it was finished. Clearly there were many with whom they did not share these privileges. I do not know if they felt that some patients could not handle it - if it was a matter of intellect - or if it was an insurance issue. I, myself, did not ask, as I did not wish to offend anyone. It is possible that they (the hospital staff) simply gave me certain liberties beyond the pale. Perhaps I should have been forced to wait with a beeping pump - an ineffectual bomb that could not quite explode - along with all the others, but they exempted me from this by teaching me how to use it.

I waited in the infusion waiting room, amid a cacophony of other people's pumps that had run down. To hear the driving alarms all around, it was hard not to jump up and shout. I was tempted to disengage the empty pumps of those around me, though I knew that I must observe more patience. This was simply another opportunity for me to grow stronger. No one may turn off all of the alarms without processing the specifics of each case.

So the noises kept going, but I was thankful. It was then that I remembered that I was pushing on, that we were not stopping there - that that was not our final resting place. We were sticking around because there were things to be done. Not large epochal events, perhaps, just simple every day events. Things that make up the day. It was worth sticking around. Not because we had to, but simply because we could.

Back at my house, I studied the wall chart. "I'm going to get him." I said to the fish. I said this to Ampoule, my nine-year-old Oscar cichlid, who was in ill-health. She was reviewing the wall chart from her tank. She flashed her tail back and forth quickly in acknowledgement of what I'd said, and then she continued to scan the chart. She was hovering above the image of The Humanist, and it was at that moment that he called.

"May His noodly appendage touch you," The Humanist said.

"May He also touch you," I replied.

We spoke of the case and of some developments. We were trying to get a bead on Melonomames, on where his headquarters might be.

"There's something on the coast I need you to check out," he said.

FIFTY THREE

Irinotecan picked me up and we headed over to check out the lobster pound.

I had gotten word that Melonomames was running his operations out of a lobster pound on The North Shore. Irinotecan and I went for lunch. It was a beautiful fall day and the sun sparkled on the water in the marshy tidal flats behind the building. We had an agent stationed outside, who was slowly changing a flat tire in the parking lot - scouting things out for us.

We were fully loaded.

Irinotecan had his stun-gun and large knife, both discretely hidden in subtle holsters beneath his vest. Rinno, as I have said before, rarely carried a regular gun. He had a motto, for the stun-gun knife combination. "Stun them and run them," he would say. And then he wouldn't say anything for a long time.

I was walking with my cane, and I had a hidden shoulder holster under my left arm. I had my portable chemo pump slung over my right shoulder - slowly pumping poison into the port in my chest. The machine functioned fully on its own. Once a minute, it rattled, like a buzzer on an old fashioned board game - as it delivered the poison. Then it clicked and was silent, until another minute had passed. Buzz, click, silence. Buzz, click, silence.

As Irinotecan and I walked past the agent, he placed two

lug nuts in front of the tire and two behind it. So, there were two henchmen out front and two in the lobster pound. I looked around to locate the henchmen out front. One was pretending to sweep out a parking space, the other was updating daily specials on a sandwich board. I nodded to Irinotecan and we stepped out of the sun into the darkness of the restaurant. Irinotecan couldn't decide between the fisherman's platter and the scallop plate. I went right for the counter where you purchase lobsters. Rinno clucked at me, as I went. He hated it when I got lobsters.

Lobster was once a food of abundance. A food for the desperate, pushed on the poorest and most downtrodden members of society - forced on both servants and prisoners. It slowly rose in both prestige and cost until it became a sign of decadent luxury. Today it has settled somewhere in the middle, provided that you live by the coast, where there are more lobsters readily available.

This is where lobster belongs, in fact, in the middle.

As the oceans rise and the water moves inland, we will all, eventually, live by the coast. If we are lucky, the lobsters will survive too, and shall remain by the coast. Perhaps, of course, if the lobsters are lucky, it is we who shall not survive. But that is another matter.

The cook had a pistol sticking out of his waistband, and I could see the outline of a holster under the apron of the cashier. Irinotecan and I sat out on the deck, drank some beers and watched the seagulls volley for scraps that the children on the deck were throwing to them.

137

Irinotecan had chosen, in the end, to go with the scallop platter. A wise choice, as it was good here. I had to hand it to the henchman in the kitchen that my lobster was cooked perfectly. It was delicious, although it had eggs along the tail. It was a female that was in the process of reproducing. They should have thrown her back when they caught her. In fact, her tail was notched, they had known better, but they had killed her anyway. It didn't matter. In a few minutes we were going to blow them all back into the ocean.

We finished our meals, and Irinotecan lit a cigarette. I laughed and said, "Cancertalkerous is going to come for you, if you're not careful." Irinotecan responded by blowing out small circles of smoke. Tiny smoke-distress signals, and I couldn't help but laugh.

Irinotecan then got up and went back inside. He walked calmly over to the fire alarm (on the wall by the men's room) and pulled it, as he passed by, continuing on his way to the kitchen. The alarm rang instantly throughout the restaurant. Women and children screamed, and all of the customers quickly filed out into the parking lot.

Sitting on the deck, alone, watching the sun play on the water, I unscrewed the sections of my cane and removed a long thin tube of explosive putty, which I molded into shape. I took the uneaten plate of fries, which had accompanied my lobster, and threw it onto the table behind me (the table closest to the door that led to and from the deck). Countless seagulls swooped down to the table, obscuring me from view. I pulled a timer and a detonator from my pocket, assembled all of the pieces, returned the charge to my pocket, and then headed for the kitchen.

As I was stepping out from the light of the deck into the darkness of the restaurant, the cashier, who was running by, saw me and stopped. He reached down underneath his apron and unsnapped his holster- as I shot him in the eye with my pellet gun. I had unsheathed the gun just prior to stepping back into the restaurant and I had surprised him. He dropped to the ground clutching his face. It was a mean thing to do, but it was only through luck and preparedness that I had prevented him from killing me. And besides, he was on the side of Cancertalkerous Melonomames, and if you are on the side of cancer, as the world is now learning, I am coming for you.

I went quickly to the kitchen. The fire alarm continued to blare. I walked around the stabbed body of the cook, at the base of the fryers, then through a doorway at the back of the kitchen, into a small office that was filled with mainframe computers and servers. The fans of the machines hummed and spun. Dozens of light emitting diodes flashed on the front panels of the servers - the wall of machines hummed. There was a stack of pornographic magazines, in the corner, with underage girls on the covers.

He was running a kiddie-porn ring.

I placed the explosive charge on the largest of the machines and returned to the kitchen. "It's time to go, Rinno!" I called, and at that moment, Irinotecan ran past me, awkwardly carrying four, large, white buckets by their handles, splashing water everywhere. The building was quiet then - except for the ceaseless din of the fire alarm.

I stepped out into the sun, in front of the building, a few paces behind Rinno. He kept running at full speed, into the center of the parking lot, and the four buckets clattered together as he ran. As Irinotecan had emerged, the two henchmen in front of the store had moved to intercept him, but the agent changing a tire had been waiting for this, and he shot both the gang members several times in the back.

The screen door to the lobster pound slammed closed behind me, and then the back of the restaurant exploded as I tapped my cane on the ground. The whole building was quickly in flames. The remaining henchmen, that we had not known of, had escaped into the marshes behind the building on inflatable speedboats. The pedestrians and diners, whose lunch had been cut short, stood and watched as fire trucks and police cars arrived.

There had been two industrious young girls dining with their mother at the lobster pound when it was destroyed. They stood outside, in the parking lot with the others, and watched as all of the emergency responders arrived to clean up. Each of the girls was carrying a handful of pens and some workbooks designed to improve math and reading skills. Irinotecan and I were standing near to them and we spoke with them for a few moments. The books were extracurricular it turned out. They were having fun sharpening up their skills with their mother at lunch. I apologized to them for blowing up the building, and pointed out the seagulls hovering in the air behind us. We talked for a little while about how clever seagulls are. How they keep themselves aloft, even in times of trouble, by conserving their energy and coasting on the different thermal currents that exist in the air, which they can sense. Then it was time for Irinotecan and I to excuse ourselves and return to the business at hand.

Rinno and I cut the bands off of the claws of the lobsters, which Irinotecan had carried out in the buckets, and we let them go in the marshy waters down behind the burning building. It was beautiful to see them go, but I had grown tired. It was silent at the edge of the water, it seemed, despite the fire behind us, except for the chemo pump slung over my shoulder. Once a minute, every minute. Buzz, click, silence. Buzz, click, silence. It was time to head home. Irinotecan dropped me off at the end of my driveway and I headed in to smoke up and eat a handful of pills.

I was closing in on Cancertalkerous Melonomames and this made me happy. I smiled to the stars on the ceiling and fell into a deep and dark oblivious sleep.

FIFTY FOUR

Perhaps you will be surprised when I tell you that I used to smoke. Perhaps you will not. We all used to smoke back in the day. I was never a prodigious smoker. I smoked half-a-pack a day, at best, and I wasn't very good at it. The cigarettes affected me strongly, and I often needed to sit down.

In the end, by the end, I was down to exactly two cigarettes a day. I spent the last three years of smoking this way. I limited myself to two a day, with the challenge that I find the best two smoking moments inherent in each day, and then smoke the cigarettes during those moments. There is a thing that non-smokers may not know about, and that former smokers may have forgotten - there are heightened moments in each day when cigarettes are, in fact, more enjoyable. They, the moments, almost always involve music, and they are often emotional, and the trick, the trick that many do not know, or possibly forget, is that you may summon them - if they do not come of their own volition. You may summon the moments.

Cigarettes are largely creatures of recollection, and are woven, perhaps inexorably, with sadness. There is something very satisfying in facing a sad recollection with a lit cigarette, a glass of something strong, and a good song. I cannot deny this. I cannot say that I did not hear the sirens calling me towards the rocks, and that I did not, at times, steer my ship slightly towards them. There is something to be said for lyrical beauty, and, many nights, I sat on the open-aired porch, in the dark, under a white string of lights (mildly drunk) listening to sad songs I had cued up to play: enjoying a singular moment, with my second and final cigarette of the day.

~

Fall was turning towards winter, and I'd let my skin get very dry. The drugs were making me break out and turn red, and I kept forgetting to put on skin moisturizer, so everything was shriveling up and cracking, turning either very red or very white. I had a head cold that I couldn't seem to get rid of, and, as I've told you previously, I couldn't seem to keep the poison off of my teeth.

Such was the process.

FIFTY FIVE

I stopped on one of the last of the beautiful days, at a
bench, beneath a small tree, downtown, just outside a
small shop that sold interesting and unusual handmade
gifts and trinkets. The store was designed to encompass
the customer, like an animal in a den. A haven of birds. It
was very comforting and was filled with treasures, and had
been named after a protective environment that an animal
creates to shield its young. I knew the owner of the store.
She was kind and I liked her. I was sitting outside this
store, on a bench, in the sun - taking it all in - when I had
the chance to speak with two adventurous young girls who
had just been inside shopping. They were standing in the
sun with their mother. And both she (their mother) and
the girls, were so beautiful. They were so beautiful. I can't
tell you how beautiful they were. But that is what they
were. There in the sun. Tall and thin, with long beautiful
hair. The little one with such marvelous curls in her hair,
and the older one looking so wise. They couldn't have
been more than five and seven. That is what they must
have been. And they were charming. They spoke with me.
They told me of the wonderful treasures they had just
purchased. She was good with them. You could see this.
You could see how well the three of them worked
together, how close they were. It was wonderful. There,
outside the store, on one of the last of the beautiful days. I
rested on the bench, far longer than I had intended, but I
was glad for having stopped.

FIFTY SIX

This is what I whisper into the blackness. This is what the Fall Rider says:

I am riding, now, fast around the corners, leaning in on the curves, coming round the bend. The leaves are churning around me and I am firing into the darkness, into the night, before it even has a chance to realize how dark it is, before it even knows that I am there. I am of the light. Of the sun. Of healing. I shall overcome the darkness that I have been presented with - simply by continuing to be. That is the secret - simply continuing to be - regardless of regardless.

FIFTY SEVEN

I stopped to visit The Artist on my way back from the hospital. I had known The Artist longer than almost any of the others. We met in elementary school and had spent our school years together, along with a small group, on the fringes of the social fabric. I had not had a chance to see him for quite some time, as the busy demands of the world had kept us occupied with other things. He and his wife were now expecting a child, and he had recently become an accountant. Becoming an accountant is always a reasonable thing to do. The Artist was often very reasonable, but I have met no other reasonable man who so appreciated the intrinsic wildness of the world all around him. Sadly, we had other ties. His mother had died at the hands of Cancertalkerous's men. We had tried to stop them, but had been unable to do so.

The Artist was raking small pebbles in a Japanese rock garden, in his backyard, when I arrived. He stopped raking as I entered the yard, and spoke to me, his eyes still cast downward upon the small pebbles, "He's come back for you," he said.

"He can have me. I'm far more trouble than he realizes," I said, and then The Artist looked up, shot me a smile, and we both laughed. He put down his rake and invited me into the house, where we sat together and drank beers, while discussing all that was going on. I would have liked to have stayed longer, but there was much to be done, and I had to get home to proceed further with my plans.

FIFTY EIGHT

I would always, when I rode my motorcycle, listen to music.* I went through a series of small cordless speaker systems that could play songs. I won't tell you the bands and songs that I listened to, as such things fall in and out of cultural stock, and usually, once they fall out, they don't return.

What you must know is that this story is not meant to be too closely chained to one form of music or another. To any one particular time. It is meant to be a future story. A story, for the future.

So, imagine your favorite songs - those are what sang out to me. That was what I heard. Those songs are what called me on. You will likely know what this is. Perhaps you can hear the songs now.

If you find that music is not spontaneously being played in your life, then, you, yourself, must make it. This might mean practicing a little every day, even when you don't feel like it. Just to stay sharp. To keep the fire going.

*I am indebted to my brother, who introduced me at an early age to the underbelly of popular music: punk and other un-commercially viable genres of music, such as anti-folk, that the larger population remains mostly unaware of. Music both strange and vital, often laced with madness, which has buoyed me up and propelled me forward, for all these many years. For the critical early awareness of such things, I am very grateful.

I could hear the speakers systems while travelling up to about 30 miles an hour. Beyond that, when I was driving between 30 and 50 miles per hour, there was nothing. I would often forget, when I got to full speed, that I had songs playing, and would be surprised by them, when I slowed down for a traffic stop. Such is the fickle nature of the brain.

It was tough, if not impossible, to get the bike up over fifty miles an hour. Driving on state and interstate highways was always a tricky business. I could legally do it. I had had to register the bike as a motorcycle, and get my motorcycle license, which I had done. I could legally do it. And I did. But it was always a tricky business. I tended to stay sharply to the right, and I spent the majority of my time (on the highways) trying to understand, and not be killed by, the wind.

FIFTY NINE

If you ever find that you must undergo a large number of medical procedures, during which you will be passing in and out of consciousness, it is important, I think, to develop a tagline or saying to mark the passage, with all its perils, from one realm to the other. As I believe that such things should be acknowledged. I will share with you, my own, as there may now be no secrets between us, if we are to make it through this together.

I did not write my own tagline, but rather it is taken from the words of the great David Bowie: from one of his earlier songs entitled *Space Oddity*. The song is about an astronaut travelling alone in space. The astronaut is speaking with people whom he has left back on earth, and right before the ship he is travelling in loses contact with those on the ground, he says, rather softly, "Tell my wife, I love her very much," to which there follows an immediate and robust full-throated response, "She Knows!"

And then communications are lost.

This is the exchange that I always shout out before losing consciousness. It is simple and straightforward, though there can be problems even with this. Sometimes they knock me out sooner than I am expecting and I only get halfway through it. Other times, anxious about losing consciousness prematurely, I will shout the whole thing out, long before I am put under, which only leads to confusion among the medical staff.

As a general rule, I will not explain what I am shouting about to the technicians prepping me for a procedure, as there is no real personal history between us, and it is not for them. To the technicians, I am largely another detail of the procedure. I do not fault them for this. But, I simply do not have the time or the energy to pull them all in.

It is to the stars that we speak.

Tell my wife I love her very much.

She knows.

SIXTY

This is what happened during my surgery.

Having called out on the table, the medical personnel circled around me. I closed my eyes and then opened them to find myself on a hilly field at the edge of the woods. Surgical prep technicians, orderlies, and anesthesiologists gathered around me, and then dispersed, as volunteers and nurses appeared in the field to help pull me up, that I may go with them.

We rose over a grassy ridge, running, the orderlies - the banner men and the banner women - with flags and surgical gauze, the nurses with pikes, and the volunteers (in their pink vests) with long, thick, wooden sticks, like those of monks. There, below us, on the other side of the knoll, they were.

There was a large group of primitive men and women, crouched down - gorging on the carcass of a deer. Its mouth and eyes had been frozen open and it cast a horrible gaze up the hill towards us. The primitive people hunched over the deer were clad in furs, but as they leapt up I saw that they were not wearing *simple* furs. They were, in fact, outfitted in fur armor. An armor covered with crushed and mutilated silver ovals: a fine and brilliant mesh armor. And they all had appropriate weapons. Thick leaden clubs and so forth.

The nurses, running in rows, both in front of and behind me, wore shiny breast-plated armor. And as we approached the wild henchmen they lowered their pikes.

Then we were upon them.

Courageous shouts and cries roared up and turned into screams. Weapons clattered and men and women fell all around me: breathing out their last. They seemed to be kneeling and doubled over, all around me. Looking quickly to the sides, I realized that the volunteers, were unarmored beneath their pink vests. They (the volunteers) were mostly older men and young women. They fought valiantly, but they had only wooden staffs, and they quickly fell - gored before me. It was at that point that I myself fell. My upper body twisted backwards on my lower body, and I fell - falling back in the direction we had run from.

My eyes started to lose their focus, but I saw The Knights emerge from the trees, galloping up the hill with enormous swords in their hands. Behind them, a row of archers emerged from the brush and released a volley of arrows. The arrows rose up to miraculous heights.

I found that I could watch nothing else.

Up, up, up, they hovered above us, and then they sank down, in an instant, into the necks and torsos of the fur clad hordes just beyond us. The Knights then rode down into the glade and, with great precision, from their horses, lopped off the heads of the remaining henchmen.

It was not long before it was over. The Knights turned and headed back toward the trees. But at the top of the hill, the last rider stopped and raised his visor. It was Dr. Aspen. He looked down to me and shouted out, "We've gotten them on the run, today, Hors. We've gotten them on the run." Then he snapped his horse's reins and galloped off.

The last of The Knights disappeared into the trees and then parking lot attendants emerged to carry the bodies off of the field. Some to be buried, some to be disposed of, as appropriate. That was the last thing I saw, as I laid my head back down.

SIXTY ONE

Here is a truth that I will now tell you. I was somewhat amazed -not that I had survived - but that I had been injured.

That the slings and arrows cast down from the heavens should actually have found their mark.

That was what startled me.

To wake up with my rectum removed. They had gotten to me. I had, to one degree or another, been gotten.

It had always been my intention to win unconditionally. But, of course, things do not always work out as we intend them.

I was ready to suffer and experience pain, I was ready for nausea (oh, how I was ready for the nausea). But, foolishly, I had thought that I would escape permanent physical injury - that the lasting scars would only be emotional.

I thought that I would escape , but they had caught up with me - and maimed me.

That was what startled me.

To look up, after being hit, hands coated in my own blood, to realize that I had been hit.

My entire mission was in jeopardy.

That was what amazed me.

~

I have a seam that runs from my testicles to my sternum. You may feel (or think) that I have misspoken. That I should have said stitches or scar (depending on the time scale from the surgery). And you would not perhaps be considered technically wrong in this. But I think of it as a seam. A visible line, showing where parts have been joined, or rejoined. A visible marker showing how the fabric is held together. A hint as to the makeup of the whole, which hints at both strength and weakness. It is both a sign of damage and of healing. There have been damages. My seams are indicators of this. I am not afraid of them or made uncomfortable by them. I shall leave that to others.

So, we must ask, what has been lost? We have lost smooth, unblemished surfaces. And there is some sadness in that. There is a wonderful silent joy in drawing fingers idly over smooth surfaces. There is something to be said for that.

But I was not, in all honesty, ever *that* smooth to begin with.

Know where your seams are, know how the whole is put together. Be not ashamed of them.

I have been battered about, and sections of the ship have been lost and destroyed.* That they (the sections) may never be used again.

*Parts of the reactor have been cordoned off, with sealed (iron) doors, that the disease may not continue to spread from one compartment to the next. Entire sections of the craft will likely remain unusable, for forever. There are concerns, at times, among the crew, that the entire vessel is no longer sea worthy. The crew is not likely wrong in this, yet we continue to head out into deeper waters (beyond the safety of the bay), on patrols in enemy territories, as there is much still to battle. I would be lying, if I said that when I give the command to dive - when I give the command to dive and I hear the dive sirens sound throughout the hull of the ship (just before we submerge), I would be lying, if I said that I do not wonder, each time, if we shall make it back to the surface. It is not for me to say, whether or not I shall make it back to the surface again. I give the command to dive, and down we go, as there are things below the surface that I must take care of. You need not follow me (below the surface) if you are uncomfortable with this. But, dear reader, we could always use another good pair of competent hands below deck. Think about it, but do not think about it for too long, as I must proceed on, with or without you. As (your) captain, I am sworn inextricably to the missions themselves. Missions I may not lay idly aside: though the obstacles before us may seem insurmountable (as they indeed might be), and though the odds are not in our favor (as they are not). We persevere. We persevere simply because we are still here. Come and persevere with me. There is still fun to be had. If you are willing to have it.

For all my falling apart, do not think, for a second, that they have gotten through to me (with their darkness and their death). They need not get through to you, either.

~

You will likely want to know what it is like to have a permanent colostomy bag, but you are not comfortable asking. I will tell you.

It is *a little bit* awful.

It is not *fully* awful. It is a little bit awful. It is manageable, but not pleasant. It is a *tiny* bit awful. It concentrates and magnifies the processed un-pleasantries of life. In addition, you must come to terms with a complete loss of control, as to how and when things happen. Lastly, you must deal with the fact that you are wholly dependent, for the rest of your life, on very specific medical supplies that are not readily available at regular stores. They must be received in the mail, and you must have them with you at all times. Sometimes, I imagine what would happen, if the supplier stopped supplying. If there was a strike, or the factories shut down.

Or if they blew them up.

Eventually, I would have to fabricate my own bags. Wax and tape contraptions, adhered to my abdomen. The logistics would be messy and difficult to work out from scratch. This may seem dark to you. But if it does, then you have not delved deeply enough into the concept behind the statement. It is, in fact, anything but dark and despairing.

I am speaking of *surviving* pointed towards *thriving*. If you cannot see yourself through to surviving, you cannot survive. It is as simple as that. You must, to a certain degree, generate yourself in your own imagination. And you should try to make a point about having a little fun with it.

But it is manageable to have a permanent colostomy bag. I will tell you more later.

SIXTY TWO

For lunch I had two hardboiled eggs and a small bag of cooked bacon. I sat at a bench, alone in the park, carefully peeled the hardboiled eggs and then placed them in the small bag of cooked bacon to salt and season them. As I ate the components of my lunch, I thought of the age of the great sailing ships - and of how they stocked and preserved their food stores for long voyages into the unknown and unexplored. I, myself, was on a long voyage into the unknown and the unexplored, and I both carefully prepared and preserved the rations I carried with me. I liked to think of all of the salted and dried goods from the great age of ships. That was what I thought of, as I ate my lunch, alone at the bench in the park.

~

There will always be warmth and small kindnesses. Do not forget this. I spend a considerable amount of time with my cat, in the evenings. PomPom sits on my lap, for hours on end, while I pet her and scratch her head. It is one of the few things that I look forward to. She is friendly and warm and quick to fall asleep, sprawled across my blanketed legs. She will often stay there for all of the night, as I keep my silent vigil, but during the day, she heads outside to hunt and kill.

As do I.

That is cat nature. You may thwart the cat, and interfere on a particular kill, but you may not change cat nature.

During the day, we both head out to hunt and kill. We hunt down the creatures foolish enough to have registered on our senses. For the cat, most often, she is chasing the sickened, weakened animals of the kingdom. As she is wont to do. While, in my case, I am hunting the sickness and the weakness of the kingdom itself.

SIXTY THREE

The majority of the bystanders I pass cannot see me. And most of those who can, see me only with contempt. It is only the younger children and the elderly who understand what I am doing. Only the littlest of children, who have no disdain for limited dreams, wave to me as I pass. It is they who can still see the magic. Surprisingly, perhaps, the elderly will often smile and wave, as well. As they, the elderly, are closer to the end, and they can intrinsically sense, on some level, that I am battling for them.

I am not loud enough, big enough, or fast enough, for anyone else to take notice, which is fine. I slip in undetected, destroy malignancy and slip out. I am the anti-tumor. The rush of white blood cells that converges to battle and then recedes away into the background, returning home when the battle is done – the larger body remains unaware of my overall adventures, yet that does not negate them. It simply means that the viewing stage is a limited one, fit only for those who have gotten word to tune in.

~

There is a complex system of simple communications among motorcyclists. The main idea is that one motorcyclist when passing another, will extend their left hand down towards the ground, at a slight angle, with an open palm, or some fingers sticking out, to acknowledge the other rider they are passing. This is a wonderful thing.

The problem is that there are many tiers of recognition and certain drivers will only acknowledge other drivers of similar types. There are very few who will return my hand signals. There are really only two groups that do. First, those on scooters, mopeds or tiny motorcycles (all of which are extremely rare creatures). Secondly, those in full gear - the survivors - who shall outlive all of the un-helmeted, un-jacketed, un-gloved, un-overpanted wreckage. The rest will have nothing to do with me. To the point that I have invented my own motorcycle signal for when I am not acknowledged. I will tell it to you now, that you may use it and spread it among the people. If you extend your open hand down and to the side, in a gesture of openness, and find that you receive nothing in return, it is very satisfying to perform a cleansing gesture. Here is what I do: I point my left hand way out, at shoulder height, away from me, and then fling my fingers to the air (to cast off the nonsense of my enemies). I then shake the filth off my hand and return it to my side. This is what I do, when other motorcyclists refuse to acknowledge me, and it always, without fail, makes me laugh.

SIXTY FOUR

There are days when I don't hunt. Days when I simply ride my motorcycle just to ride it. When I walk just to walk. There are days when I remember that it is just play. Shifts of tone are needed. We may not always speak with the same voice. We must make different sounds at different times. There are irreverent days. Days when the vial in my cane is filled with pure nonsense. Days on which I may better sense the weather. Days when the light of clarity shines especially bright around the edges of everything. When the fall air can, in fact, sparkle with the crackle of the sunlight itself. The moment, when, if you are watching, you may see the light of the sun move around the edges of an object and see it pass, from the one object onto the next. The transfer of light and heat. Beams of light travelling 93 million miles just to be here. Just to be. There are still those days too. But we may not focus on those days here, as we have a different tale to tell.

SIXTY FIVE

The walk to the hospital was always tremendous. It is as far as you think. I had to cross many cities and towns, find many ways over and around many highways. It almost didn't seem possible. The first time I walked to the hospital it seemed almost fantastical. Something strange out of an old story, an old fable, an old myth. It was too much. But somehow it was manageable, and I did it.

But, mostly, I rode my motorcycle to the nearby commuter rail station, and then took the commuter rail into the city. The hospital is only a short walk from the commuter rail station. That is what I most often did.

SIXTY SIX

I'm not sure how, but one morning a large number of gang members breached the security perimeters of the hospital and made it all the way up to the waiting room for the chemo-infusion ward. They showed up during high-traffic, around 10 in the morning, when everyone was about to be let in and setup for a bed (for the day). Irinotecan and I hadn't gotten there yet, as I wasn't due in that morning until later. I don't know if I have told you this before, but it's mostly older folks waiting for chemotherapy. Almost everyone is elderly, except for myself and a few others.

That day they really got the elderly. They slashed up a lot of old men and women, and shot a bunch of others. Many were killed. It was bad. It was really bad. They were triaging the victims right there in the waiting room when we arrived. There was a horrendous amount of blood, and everywhere we looked there seemed to be bandaged old men and women moaning. Things were escalating. We were going to need to reel it all in quicker than I had expected.

But during the battle that had taken place in the waiting room, the hospital staff had managed to kill several of the gang members, and Rinno and I helped place the bodies of the aggressors on stretchers and wheel them outside. As I was loading one of the last ones on, he startled me by coughing. He didn't open his eyes, but I could tell that he could hear me. I pushed him along the hallway on the gurney. As I walked, I leaned over and whispered to him,

165

"You, sir, are a plastic bag filled with water based cleanser that women occasionally use to clean their nether regions with. And your time is almost up. You shall soon be malignant no more. I need do nothing more to you, now. You are away from your host. You have already sustained injuries that shall take you. I shall simply wheel you out into the open air and leave you there - that you may reflect for a few moments on how you have chosen, before you die. You have chosen incorrectly in the battle of wrong and right. Think of how you have allowed what was good within you to mutate, to become a pathogen. Ponder how you have allowed a frenzied orgy of malignant cellular production. You chose this. And you may not *now* be separated from it. But you may die with one virtue. You may now know, in your heart of hearts, that you *should* have chosen otherwise. As you feel the rays of the sun on your face this morning, as I wheel you outside, to your death, you shall know this. That is what I leave you with. If there is anything good left within you, you will own that. Own that before you go. Know that you have failed. Feel the sun on your face, and turn it toward the light."

The gang member said nothing, but gasped and wheezed sharply, as I stepped away from the stretcher to return to the building behind me.

SIXTY SEVEN

As I have said before, I was never an officer of the law. Though I do fight for things, now, and uphold certain universal laws. I am an officer *now* of right and wrong, of light and dark, and I walk the line between them. My shadow falls on both sides. I am welcome to the left and to the right, but I try to keep my course steady in the middle. Although things are not always clear and one-sided.

Time passed. Though we had blown up his headquarters, we could not locate Cancertalkerous Melonomames to finish the job. I searched. I hunted. But I grew sicker and more tired, and more and more time passed. I developed a nasty cough and a relentless head cold, on top of everything else. I became somewhat despondent. There were days I chose not to get out of bed. I smoked and drank a lot, and thought and thought and thought. At some point, I began to shut down a bit, without really realizing it. I gave up, a little, inadvertently. The weather was beginning to turn. It was turning then to winter, and I was forced to realize that I would soon need to put the motorcycle away for the season. Though it would still be ready. The gas tank full, complete with a gasoline stabilizer. The battery plugged into a maintenance charger, the bike would be ready to go at a moment's notice, but I knew that I would not be riding it for some time. I, perhaps, would not be ready (to go).

Ampoule, the fish, was only eating intermittently. My only true recourse in getting her better was to perform massive water changes. There is nothing better for a fish than a large influx of fresh water - provided it is the correct temperature and that it has been treated to neutralize the chlorine and the chloramines (from the tap water). But even massive water changes, which had always proved to be a balm for any illness when the fish was younger, seemed to do little then. Though I still performed them, as it was all I knew to do. The only weapon I had.

~

There is a good chance that I shouldn't be imprisoning fish. That it is wrong to do so. I think about this often. I have always striven to provide the best possible environments. To provide the best conditions and the largest aquariums that money and space may allow. But the largest cage is still a cage. It bothers me. It bothers me. An irritant that will not go away. To limit a fish's ability to swim freely. While it is not a crime on the level of denying a bird flight, it is perhaps, still, a serious crime. One that I am guilty of. There is something to be said for swimming. There are crimes of which I am guilty, for which I must someday pay.

And I will, I will pay.

SIXTY EIGHT

After the waiting room attack, things went downhill quickly. I don't know if I have mentioned it before, but one aspect of Chemagi's therapy was that I developed an extreme sensitivity to cold. Whenever I touched metal I could feel it, even at room temperature, burning into my skin like electricity. Cold water was incredibly intense. I had to wash my hands in warm and hot water exclusively, to avoid stunning myself into a mild shock. I must give Cancertalkerous credit, as his men knew this. They caught me unawares one day in the far bathroom of the chemo-infusion ward. I had walked down to the bathroom at the end of the corridor, as the other bathrooms were in use.

It was a bathroom unique to the ward, in that it had a small shower station installed in the corner. I believe that they used it to hose down patients who had experienced bad allergic reactions to the various drugs (as a lot of patients seemed to have bad reactions), but I don't really know.

I don't know why there was a shower station installed, but that bathroom was the only one available, so that was the one I used. There were two gang members: one in the corner behind the door, pointing a gun at me, and the other smashing my head up against the wall. He knocked my head against the wall for so long that I found that I was beginning to lose track of having my head knocked against the wall. Then he turned on the cold water in the sink and pushed my hands and face down into the water. I found that I could not help but cry out from the incredible sharpness of the cold.

SIXTY NINE

Irinotecan burst through the door and knocked the gang member who had been restraining me across the room. The henchman hit the shower wall and slid down it, unconscious. But Rinno hadn't seen the other standing behind the door. That man shot Rinno three times in the back.

He shot him in the back as he had been helping me up. And everything stopped. Irinotecan had been lifting me up from the ground. He had me half-way up when he was shot, and he stopped and looked at me with such a strange look on his face, such a strange look of gentle surprise, like a child who had just discovered something he couldn't quite believe - and then he lowered me slowly back down, as he himself sank towards the floor.

He had been so vibrant. He had allowed for the very continuation of my own existence, but he was leaving me, and all I could do was look up at him.

There was a large commotion around us as people streamed into the room to restrain the two gang members, but I couldn't really see any of them. Irinotecan then said to me, "This is as far as I can take you. You must go the rest of the way without me."

He smiled sadly and continued, "My name is Irinotecan, and I am a member of the CPT-11 Clan. I have watched out for you, but I am no longer able to be effective. I can do no more. May you find all the resolution you need to find, peacefully, in the end." And that was it. He was gone.

I had never been more alone.

I vomited on the floor as an overpowering wave of nausea hit me. It took me a long time to sit up, but eventually I did.

The nurses and orderlies, on our side of the light, removed the gang member who'd been knocked into the wall. But then there was the matter of the other, the one who had shot and killed Irinotecan.

On my instructions, they handcuffed Rinno's shooter in the shower stall, turned on the water, and left. The water ran and ran, and I sat quietly by Irinotecan's body.

He had fallen and would not rise again. We had been good friends, but I had not been able to save him.

"I am damaged, but functional," I said to the air. "We shall fight on - through to the end."

I reached for Irinotecan's knife, but then stopped and removed the stun-gun from its holster instead. I disabled the stun gun's safety mechanism, stood unsteadily and limped over to the shower stall, as the stun-gun crackled in my hand. The water ran and ran. "It could have been worse," I said to the shooter, whose eyes were darting around wildly. "I was going to cut you into tiny pieces for a full lab analysis. But, we shall do this instead." I stopped just short of the shower stall and tossed in the crackling stun-gun and then turned to leave.

It was horrible, even though I had intended it.

It was horrible and then it was done. I dragged myself back to the treatment room where I sat, quite quiet and quite still, in the chair, in the dark, for a very long time.

At one point, the intercom snapped on, and Chemagi began to speak over the line, "Mr. Patient, I pose this riddle to you, from a common fortune cookie, 'How dark is dark? How wise is wise?'"

But I don't know what he said beyond that - because I pulled the cord out from the intercom, and the only thing after that was static.

Rinno was dead.

My treatment was over.

I left the hospital with intentions not to return. I could not shake the coldness of the night, and my arms and legs shook violently the entire way home.

SEVENTY

I will beat Death. I will not defeat Death, as that is not possible. But I will beat Death about the face and hands when I find him. Death knows this, and has been avoiding me.

~

This is the credo I repeat aloud as I ride:

"Irinotecan is gone. I am beyond Irinotecan. I am Hors. I am post cancer. I am the balm for the wounded. I am The Fall Rider. I roll now over the black ground hunting on my motorcycle with the bright yellow light of the sun. If you are the embodiment of sickness itself, I am coming for you. I will fall but rise again. And when I no longer rise, others shall rise behind me, as the sun. I am coming around the bend, right now, at high speed, as the leaves churn around me. My gun is already drawn and I am firing into the darkness, before the darkness has even had a chance to realize how dark it actually is - before it has even had a chance to discern that I am actually there. I will take illness by surprise and cast it back to the winds from whence it came. The annals of ill-health will know my name. There shall be hope for the injured and protection for the maimed."

I am The Fall Rider. Complacency shall not remain. We shall join forces and grow well again.

~

How dark is dark? How wise is wise?

Very. Very.

~

There are times when you will find yourself in jams.
Things will seem insurmountable. The option to crash and
burn will hover itself before you. But you do not need to
choose it. If you are wise, you will adopt the way of the
motorcyclist. (It does not matter whether or not you have
ever physically ridden a motorcycle, so long as you know
the way. I will tell it to you, now, as it is something that all
drivers must learn as they become motorcyclists. It is not a
secret, it is written about plainly in manuals and
handbooks on motorcycle riding, but you might not know
it, and so I shall explain it here.)

When you encounter an obstacle, when you find yourself
at the edge of a serious accident that is unfolding around
you, as the accident unfurls before you (like the petals of a
flower) as your sense of time slows down, and you realize
that you are in the middle of it, do not resign yourself to
disaster. Do not throw your arms up in desperation. Keep
them (your hands) down on the handlebars that control
the vehicle, and look for a way through. There is almost
always a way through, but you must know to look for it.
Though you may find yourself surrounded by enormous
hulking vehicles and objects, both mobile and immobile,
although you may find yourself surrounded by enormous
sliding machines, sparking on the ground, do not forget
that you are light and quick - you are small, fast and deft.
You are a motorcyclist, after all, and you may adjust your
course far more readily than those around you. See a way

through and then follow it. You shall outmaneuver your opponents and escape into the night, to live to see the morning sun again. This is something I ask of you. This is something I ask. So much of it is done in the mind.

SEVENTY ONE

I have not addressed, for quite some time, the elaborate chart that I constructed and then hung on the wall, to study the gang and track my efforts to stop them. I have not mentioned it as I stopped working on it after Rinno died.

One day I came home, and I didn't have it in me.

I had made some new identifications of gang members, which I needed to represent on the board, but I didn't have it in me. I stared at the board. I stared and stared at the board. And I just didn't have it in me anymore to update it: so I stopped. I left the clippings in a pile on the floor. And soon after that I stopped cutting out the clippings all together.

~

Ampoule seemed to be having a harder and harder time eating the pellets at the surface of the water. Each day it was worse, and it troubled me.

SEVENTY TWO

I had three, large, raw, Portobello mushrooms for lunch. There is a wonderful texture and sensation to biting through the cap of a large, raw mushroom. The difference of the spongy upper side of the cap, juxtaposed with the gentle gills underneath. This is what I had for lunch. You may know that mushrooms are, in fact, a carcinogen. It seems, at times, that almost everything in this world is a carcinogen. Anyway, I welcome it. I say, let it be drawn. Let Him be drawn to me. Let Him come to me. Let Him find me.

This is what I say to Him. This is what I say aloud to the air, "Understand that I stand here, as a Man, to draw you out. Come to me now - that we may square off - and have it out. One of us to walk away. One of us to not. I am power. I am empowered. I am empowerment. And I call out to the darkness, now. Do not waste your time with others. Come now for me. And see what you shall find."

SEVENTY THREE

The Conversationalist called me. I have always enjoyed talking with her, as she has a wonderful sense of humor and a tremendous recall of the details that make up an event, and she is able to pull them forth at any moment. Bringing them to the fore in a way that is both funny and true. She is able to evoke the words, the expressions and the inflections of the events and stories from our group of friends from long ago. Many in the group are able to do this to one degree or another, but she is exceptional at it. I, myself, in juxtaposition, have always had trouble remembering more than the general gist of many of the stories, even the ones in which I am predominantly featured. It is only a few stories that I have told and retold incessantly, which have stuck with me. There is nothing to be done for this. It simply is what it is. And so, I enjoy the memory of others. There are one or two stories that I do remember, however, and perhaps I shall tell one or two of them to you, but first we must talk about The Fisherman.

The Fisherman was the first in our group to die. He had died fifteen years earlier, at the age of twenty-five. He was one of the only people I have known personally, who has died - whose death was not directly related on some level to Cancertalkerous and his men. He drowned, and The Conversationalist and I discussed, how, had he not died all those years ago, he would have recently turned forty years old. The Fisherman had been equal parts, funny, intelligent, gregarious, and endearing, and he had met, befriended and genuinely engaged more people in his short

179

life, than anyone else I have ever known.

He also had a remarkable and uncanny ability, to let you
know, as a friend, when you were being an asshole, in a
way that was earnest and true - in a way that was bracing,
but not too bracing, in a way that I have not found in
another person. He often had to tell me that I was being a
bit of an asshole, as I'm afraid that I often was a bit of an
asshole, back then, and I am thankful that he was able to
say so. He would find it tremendously funny, now, that I
no longer physically have an asshole.

We all missed him, and as I spoke with The
Conversationalist, I tried to imagine what it would be like
had he not died, but I could not.

I have said The Fisherman's death was not directly affected
by Melonomames, and this is true, but Melonomames
killed his father. It was a long and protracted death - drawn
out over many years. Cancertalkerous's magic destroyed
his mouth and throat and then ate away at his face - taking
his very jaw. But The Fisherman's father was stoic and true
and he remained strong all the way to the end. One of the
crueler aspects of all this was the fact that The Fisherman's
father had been an expert chef and a gourmet, who took
great pleasure in food - the particular attacks of
Cancertalkerous Melonomames had ruined his ability to
enjoy such things by destroying his very jaw, mouth and
throat. The Fisherman's mother is still alive, though she
has lost both men and must carry forward without them.
She is strong and true, and I still speak with her. It is for
her, and for the others who have lost so much that I ride.
She understands why I fight. Why I fight the malignancy

through the days and the nights. It is for her and others like her that we must uphold the power of healing and reparation - that we must pull ourselves together the best we can - that we must nurse the ill and the sickly back to full health - that they may stand again in the sun and run alongside the river. We shall make whole that which has been damaged - make whole that which has been undone. We shall lift up the downtrodden, until they themselves stride along with us, powerful and well - bright points of light in the winter sky.

We must remain valiant and strong and fight on, for now at least, regardless of the sadness and the sickness that we may feel - we must continue on - despite the sores and the rashes and the nausea - as beyond the aches and pains is something beautiful.

~

Though they may continue to take pieces of us away - chipping away at our malignancy - we must not let ourselves feel diminutive - we will always be, in the summation of whatever parts we have left - greater than the whole. We are the bright points of winter light - shining in opposition to the darkness. And there is no darkness that cannot be broken by even the smallest beam of light.

I have told you that I have trouble recounting the critical details that make up the specifics of the stories of long ago - the details that make up my life - and this is no lie. I shall tell you now a brief and partial story, that goes nowhere, of The Fisherman and I from twenty years ago.

We lived together, for a year, as roommates (in the dorms), during college, and we spent many long hours drinking together and laughing. One night, in our room, we were playing an involved computer game - one which required the establishment, and lengthy nurturing of complex fictional characters, who together in a small group fought the evil around them. The characters grew and developed, acquired things and battled within the world of the game. We were both deeply drawn to the game and had only, that night, come to realize that the characters we had carefully developed had drawn us too far from the immediate world around us. We had been leaving our room, to see others, far less than we should have. So, that night, when we played, we played carelessly and allowed all of the characters to die - ending the game for us, which was tremendously liberating. It was agreed between us that we would not return to an earlier save point, or begin the game anew. We had played the game and now we were done. We would return our attention to the world around us.

After the game was over and the computer off, The Fisherman picked up two empty wine glasses from a shelf on the wall and poured the final dregs of a cheap bottle of wine into our glasses. He gave us each a glass and then explained the game that we were to play. (I believe that the game had a clever name, but I must leave it out, as I don't remember it.) The Fisherman, who was five years later to drown, told me the simple basis of the game.

I had just been given the last sip of wine in the world - there would be no more forever for anyone. And he wanted, simply, to know what I would do with it. How would I drink it? Would I drink it rapidly or slowly? Would I give it away to someone? Or do something else? He told me how he had played the game before, with other friends over the years, and he told me some of the responses and reactions that people had had, which were interesting, but I must apologize, as I do not remember the specifics, and I cannot recount them here. I do not even remember The Fisherman's own solution to the problem, which saddens me, as I would like to know it, but there is nothing to be done for that now. I am embarrassed to say that, selfishly, I only remember my own solution.

I raised my glass, with the world's last sip of wine, to the light, to properly examine and appreciate it, and I brought the glass grandly towards my lips, but just before it reached my mouth, I stopped and threw it as hard as I could against the far wall of our room where it hit the door and shattered into countless pieces. There was something tremendously satisfying in that, and it was a long time before we stopped laughing. We left the glass, with all its shards, where it was on the floor. We would deal with it in the morning.

~

Dear reader, it is almost ridiculous what you will do. All of the wonders that shall unfurl. You have a special challenge, and I give it to you now. It appears that the oceans are acidifying and rising, right now.

It is going to get bad.

Things are going to get bad, but it does not mean that we may never return to a good future. So long as fascists do not shout our slogans from their loud speakers, if we are just able to keep the words to the everyday, just to keep (everything) on the everyday, then we shall do just fine.

Of course, it is also possible that you will need to shout things out of speakers.

Nothing is entirely clear now. Nothing is entirely simple. Go forth, and no matter what, tell stories of the stories of it, to the little ones. Spread words and keep things interesting. Don't give up, unless you must. There is always a small something to be said for giving up. Everything does not win on forever. And if you forget that, you will be more sad than you need be, when the time comes.

Fight hard and be true, until it is time to give up. There is something to be said for that. If you can see only one side of the line, you lose all perspective. You lose all depth. Look to the center. Remember the hard stone center that has threatened to break our teeth, should we approach it incorrectly. Remember that center, appreciate its danger, then approach it all the same.

SEVENTY FOUR

I went to the stay with The Engineer for a few days. He
lived then in the city. (We all went to school together: The
Engineer, The Fisherman, The Humanist, The
Conversationalist, The Teacher and I. The Artist had gone
to a different university, but he had hung out with us
during the summers. It was a good group, and there were
many more people of course, many more good people, but
I can't capture them all here.)

The Engineer had recently gotten divorced, his wife had
turned into a different person who could no longer love
him, and he was coming to terms with that. He lived in a
gorgeous, large house that they had once lived in together.
We had spoken years ago, The Engineer and I, when he
was alone and single. We had made tentative plans then to
have him live on a small plot of undeveloped land, which
my family had owned by the ocean. The land was unsettled
and heavily wooded and it overlooked a steep, rocky cliff
that pitched down to the edge of the ocean. We were
going to build a yurt, which is circular form of a tent, used
by nomadic people. The idea was that The Engineer would
live alone in the yurt and work on various forms of
mechanical devices, at his leisure, over the years. The first
device though would have to be a small catapult, and with
it he would cast into the ocean small trinkets of his past
that had become troubling. Whenever we would visit, we
would all bring small trinkets of our own that had become
troubling, and we would catapult them all into the sea.
Then we would sit on logs, roughly hewn from trees, and

185

nestle around the warmth of the fire, at the center of the yurt. The heat would radiate out to us all. We would tell stories, both old and new, and make plans for the future.

This never happened. I wish, on many levels, that it had. The real house The Engineer had was quite nice though, and it suited him. So, perhaps it was for the best that it worked out as it did. In addition, I needed a place to stay for a while, as my house was being watched, and The Engineer was one of my only friends who had his own full pellet gun range (in his basement). We said our hellos, grabbed several cans of beer and headed down to his range to practice.

Sometimes, I am bad, and I make people uncomfortable. It is tough when a long term relationship ends. It is hard to see through to the potential of the future - it takes a tremendous amount of patience and time and hope. Sometimes, I tell things to The Engineer that he does not necessarily want to hear, but I think that they are important, so I tell him anyway.

Before I drifted off to sleep that night, guided by several beers and a large number of anti-nausea pills, I said to The Engineer, "It may take quite some time, but you are generally well liked by all that know you, and it is very likely that you will fall in love again. More likely than not you will fall into a deep and mutual, reciprocal love within this lifetime. It is *possible* that it won't happen, of course, but I think that *that* is unlikely."

I say that to all of you, dear readers, as well. No matter what happens, you will fall in love again, if you let yourself.

Do not forget that.

SEVENTY FIVE

I went to the park and sat on the far bench in the late afternoon. Children came and went: fluttering in and out of the park, with their parents and guardians. The last of them left as dusk fell. Normally, I would have stood and returned to my home then, but I found that I simply did not have it in me. So I stayed, sitting on the bench, well into the darkness.

There are real vampires in the world, but they are not what most people think. They are ticks. They are the ticks that sit patiently on the edges of leaves and blades of grass. Right there, in that park. Waiting, patiently, for a host. There is a tick population explosion occurring right now, which will likely not abate for many years to come. Nothing carries so many diseases and pathogens so lightly. The seeds of so much ill-health, hidden so cleverly in so tiny a frame. So much darkness, which often slips by undetected, until it is too late. So many of us will be infected in the years to come. But we will deal with it, I guess, the best that we can.

I sat in the park, as the ticks slowly climbed onto my legs.

The stars finally emerged above me, and I tilted my head up to see them. It was then that Cancertalkerous Melonomames stepped forward from the darkness behind me, placed a rope over my neck and pulled me up by it, up off the bench, up towards the night sky. I was unable to turn or run. And I wasn't completely sure that I wanted to.

He raised me slowly and strongly up into the air. Instinctually, I grasped at the rope with my hands and kicked my feet a little bit. But then I let go a little. I let my legs relax, and I brought my arms down to my sides, as I continued to watch the stars. Melonomames grunted and leaned in close to my ear, and then whispered something. He said, "So, you have children, eh? And a pretty wife, eh? Pretty, pretty, pretty."

And that was it.

No.

No.

No.

He would not. I would not let him. He and his men would not get to them. I would keep them safe. That was the one thing I would do. I would keep them out of all of this, and I would keep them safe. At all costs, I would keep them safe. I had kept them safe until now and I would keep them safe for all time.

Cancertalkerous Melonomames whispered insidious little things deep inside my ear, as he pulled the rope tighter, but I did not hear the things that he said. In fact, he, himself, began to have trouble hearing the things he said, as I reached back to the farthest reaches of darkness, back behind my own head, to his, and with the strength of the gods, tore off his ears.

SEVENTY SIX

I had reached down through the darkness, through the heart of hearts. Past all of the sadness and heartbreak. (The mother zebra who mourns the loss of her foal - standing by the body of her child for days more than she should. Protecting her baby, even in death, from the ravages of the world.) I reached past all of the anger. (The wild-eyed father who tracks down the killer of his child - beating the killer to death with his bare hands until there is nothing left but the bloodied and raw remains of both himself and his opponent.) Past all of the ravages of sickness. (The torment, all of the torments of the body. The pain and discomfort of all of the crippling fevers and disfigurements that wither the body and claw at the soul.) Past all of those who must tend the sick and the dying. (Their hearts torn asunder with the knowledge that sometimes they may do nothing more than be present and dab at perspiring foreheads with washcloths of sorrow.) It is worse to witness the ravages, than to be ravaged. It is then that one may catch a glimpse through doorways of infinite sorrow. (Though these are doors we must never open.) I reached down and backwards through all of this, as it swirled around me, flashing like stars - there in the park, in the darkness. It was there that I reached out and pulled off the ears of my nemesis. It was there that I broke through the sadness of tomorrow and ravaged the ravager. It was there, in that moment, that I left - travelling to places that you may not follow.

Cancertalkerous Melonomames reeled backwards,

dropping myself and the rope. He reached his hands up to the sides of his head - and unleashed an unearthly howl. I struggled to my feet, gasping, wheezing, and unable to speak. I began what would be a very long, slow, walk home, stumbling and lurching in the dark, a rasping, gasping, half-monster/half-man, on the verge of nothingness.

Behind me, Cancertalkerous Melonomames crouched down, picked up his bloodied ears from where they had fallen, and ran off into the night, like an animal. Howling as he ran.

He would not hear me coming, next time, perhaps, but he would know, *now*, that I am, in fact, coming for him.

I would not be able to see my girls again. I could expose them to no further danger.

SEVENTY SEVEN

She called me the next day. The day after I tore off Cancertalkerous's ears. It was so rare that we got to talk then, it was so sad, and so unfortunate that we were both upset. I missed her terribly. She knew that Cancertalkerous had gotten through to me, that He now knew both of her presence and that of the children.

I had failed. It had not been my intention. All I could tell her was that I would do whatever I could to bring things to an accelerated conclusion. And that I loved her. That was all I could do.

It is never enough. You can never curl up with your children *enough times* that they will no longer need you to curl up with them again. There is no set number of times. It is never enough, and you must deal with that. That is all there is to it. It is never enough.

SEVENTY EIGHT

When I sit up, properly, on my motorcycle, when I ride with the visor fully up, when I raise my chin, proudly, to bring it level with the ground - it is then that I can hear the banshees. I hear the banshees crying on the wind. It is a beautiful, disturbing sound. I acknowledge them silently and then lower my head back down, to silence their cries, as I am not yet ready for them.

And they are not yet ready for me.

For the lesson is this: fears and weaknesses aside, we *may* still be tremendous forces, should we simply choose to be. And I, for one, have not yet given up. A good portion of being alive, is embracing conflict, in one form or another, in one way or another. I, myself, to be honest, am not very good with conflict. I am not very good at many things, in fact. But I am tenacious. I am tenacity. I am The Fall Rider, and I am coming around the bend now, with the leaves churning behind me, firing into the darkness, before the darkness has even had a chance to discern that I am there, before it has even realized how dark it actually is. You shall ride with me. We will cast sickness and ill-health back into the winds from whence they came. They shall know of us, in the annals of ill-health. We shall ride with the brightness of the sun. We shall sing. We shall sing loudly: tremendous songs of great and terrible things.

~

Whenever I cross The Merrimack River on my motorcycle,

I have always looked to it, to check its status. To date, no matter what, it has always been beautiful.

SEVENTY NINE

I am not running out of time. I am here, in this moment. I have what I need, and am reaching out to you. Sounding, sounding, sounding: radar in the dark. We are always here, in the moment. All you must do is be aware of it. But, of course, if you are not – that's fine too.

You may do all that you need, right here and now.

~

I am tired today. A little worn down. I am not sure that I am up for it. I do not think that *it* is up for me. No matter, we shall plod on and wade through. We shall wade through it, holding our weapons high, up above the water, that they may be ready (clean and dry) should we need them. Ready should we need to turn and fire.

Some days you must plod along, half submerged in the mire. In thorough discomfort. Water constantly in your boots, the threat of various skin diseases running along your wet skin. Surrounded, perhaps, by unseen enemies - enemies all around and possibly within you. There are unperceivable traps hidden everywhere– at the edges of the jungles and the desserts, along even the well tended paths that lead through the fields and forests. You may be snared. You may get trapped. Do not settle for this though. Push through, regardless.

Plod on. The day shall eventually catch fire with the light and the warmth of the sun. (I need you) to capture that warmth, to capture it, and carry it along to others. That it (the warmth) may spread.

~

There were rumors that Cancertalkerous's lineage went all the way back. All the way back to the origins of cancer itself. It was crazy, of course. Highly unlikely, at best. But then again, what if it was true? What if it was true and we were able to disrupt the chain by destroying him. I couldn't get this thought out of my mind.

They said that he was tied directly back to the beginning. That there had been an unbroken line of malignancy, in which, no matter how thin the chain had gotten, it had never broken. The link was now thin. If I could get to him and disrupt the chain. Who knew, maybe it could work. Maybe I could stop it all.

I didn't know. But it was all I had.

I was going to disrupt him. I was going to disrupt the chain. I was going to cut the chain into pieces.

I had been resting, one afternoon, on a bench to regain my energy but then I was ready to stand and go again, so I stood and went. I walked home and rested. I went upstairs and lay down in the darkness.

"He doesn't fully know who's after him," I said to the air, and I laughed maniacally in the dark.

I couldn't sleep and I didn't get the rest I needed, but it didn't matter. Once your body has really decided on something, you don't need the same amount of rest. Once

your body has resigned itself to getting something done,
you get what you need, and that's it.

~

I have come to realize that the cat and I are more similar
than I initially realized. She is shy and timid.

She is not a cat's cat.

She keeps to herself. She cowers in the yard, if another cat
enters it.

And yet she can chew the head off a chipmunk. She is an
efficient, powerful killer. And she does what she needs to
do. But she is shy.

We are both powerful but flawed.

In this way, we are alike.

EIGHTY

I have told you, previously, that I would tell you what it is like to have a permanent colostomy bag, though I have not yet gone into it in any real depth. I will do so now. It is manageable. That is most important. Above all, it is manageable. But there is a certain indignity to it. Incontinence has about it, a certain end-of-life air. In general, the control of one's own bowels is (normally) one of the final controls to be given up. One of the final things to go. I know that there are exceptions to this, but that is the general rule. (Please note that I anticipate angry letters from well adjusted individuals who have colostomy bags, but have come to terms with them. I will do my best to respond to all your letters.)

It is odd to not have control of your own bowels. To simply experience them perform, within a system of medical apparatuses, when and how they please - to hope that things go well. I wear a medical device that is attached to my body at all times. The system rarely fails, but there is always the sense that it could. You are always only one moment away from experiencing a system failure. A moment away from a breach. You are constantly riding the edge of potential failure.

The device, or the *appliance*, as the medical staff call it, must be worn at all times, though it is never clear when it will be needed. There is no reprieve from it. You may never really take it off, as you never know what is going to happen. The replacement parts, the bags and bases that make up the device are not available locally at any store. You must purchase everything ahead of time, remotely, and then wait for the pieces to arrive. And you must take the supplies with you everywhere you go.

The supplies are not something you may run out of.

To simply run low on supplies is extremely stressful. It is manageable, but wearying, as there is no downtime. It is what it is. And that is that.

I miss the parts that were taken from me. I miss my rectum and anus. In addition to the anus, they took, as they had to, all of the musculature that controls the region, that which once allowed me control. Now there is nothing.

I can manage it, as I have said, but I will simply reiterate that there is a small indignity to it all. To lose control of this particular feature, is to lose control over one of the basics. To lose control, permanently, of one of the fundamental aspects of one's own biology: a loss that normally only occurs at the very end of one's life cycle - to lose control early and prematurely is dispiriting.

I would be lying if I did not admit that at times it makes me feel as though I am approaching my own end.

Though, to be clear, we are not, in the end, dispirited by it. We are not. We do not allow ourselves to be, as there are many things to do. And we must do them, and we shall. We will not slow down. We will not waver. We will not hesitate or fail to complete the missions in front of us. We carry on, and we shall predominate despite the presence or hindrance of any such appliances or devices. In fact, we will work harder to prosper - directly because of the presence of such things - because of them. We shall work harder.

I only mention that it can be dispiriting, as this is a true and clear aspect of its real nature, and not to acknowledge it would only be to empower it further. We are not afraid. We are not afraid, here, to examine things and call them as they really are.

We persevere. We persevere until we will no longer persevere, and then, that is that.

~

What does my stoma look like? It looks like a small raspberry volcano. Though it does not usher up lava. No, it does not usher up lava. It maintains an active status. Though it is frequently dormant, you may never count on "the where" and "the when" of its dormancy. It is best for the villagers to keep their distance. Lest it kill them all. It is stoic but can punish mercilessly - erupting on a sudden whim.

EIGHTY ONE

In truth, I was never a very good mechanic. I had always fluttered anxiously around the peripheral systems of the motorcycle, tightening the chain, changing bulbs, switching out the spark plug, and adjusting small things here or there, but there was much about the engine that I didn't really understand. There were many components of the engine that were beyond both my physical reach and my conscious understanding. Things that I simply counted on to do what they were designed to do. (In much the same way, that I counted on the various processes of my own body to do what they were designed to do - my lungs to breathe, my heart to pump blood, etc. etc.)

~

The bike had a critical system failure on the way home from the hospital. It was the last day I had planned on riding it that season. I was only a mile from my home, and the seams just came apart. I was at the last major turn, by the convenience store, on the way to my house - when the rear sprocket that had held the motorcycle's chain to the back wheel assembly came loose, which caused the chain to fly off and cut through all of the components around it. The bolts that had held the sprocket down had all come loose or been sheared off.

I had to walk the bike, with its mangled back end, the rest of the way home. When I got it into the garage I studied where the bolts had been and realized that I had missed them. I had missed them, somehow, years before, when I had taken off all the bolts and locked them down, so long ago, by adding washers and special sealants. I had missed these bolts and they had released their charge, the very sprocket that had held the chain in place, the very chain that had allowed the bike to run, and the chain had torn through the bike at speed - devastating it. The bike would run no more.

I had walked the bike the final mile home, and pulled it into the garage and then it was done. The bike was done. It had come, and it had gone. It had come, and I had maintained it, and then it was done. I could no longer do it. Too much had gone wrong. I no longer had it in me. I had failed. Do not misunderstand me; I did not fully give up on it right away, not right then and there, not that day, but later. I spent hours and hours - I spent days - trying to replace all of the damaged parts and pieces - the bolts, the sprockets, the molding, and countless other small pieces. I phoned endless mechanics and searched international websites until my eyes could no longer read, and I could no longer stand it. But it was too much, and I knew it. The parts were too specific, too hard to find, and no matter where I looked, I could not find what I needed to make it run again. The bike would never run again. It was beyond my level of ability. It was done. It was done, and it was hard for me. It was hard when it finally set in.

EIGHTY TWO

The fall had rushed in from the summer, and before I knew it, it too was ending. The weather had held remarkably, with the days seeming to hold an unfathomable amount of warmth and light. The air was clear and clean, and the sun seemed to shine on me far more than it should have, so late in the season. Then the last fall day had come and gone, and now, somehow, winter had arrived. We had reached the solstice, our darkest day, tilted away from the light.

I did not mind, though, the transition, as much as I had expected. My energy was low, but I had come to a place of relative peace. I'd given up on the bike, and stopped chasing the gang so much - I was only reading reports on them on occasion. I had recently ordered some small trinkets online, and they were due to arrive that very day. The arrival of the trinkets was helping to focus my attention onto warmer, more positive, quieter matters, and I looked forward to their receipt. I did chores around the house and was at peace.

~

What a wonder it is to wash a few dishes in the sink, by hand. No soap, no need for soap. Nothing's as dirty as you think, in that everything is *a little* dirty.

But what a wonder it is to turn the glasses carefully under the water. To rub off the sediment and the filth, the food particles, with my fingers. (Wiping down the sink is my

Chinese rock garden.) To watch my hands move so freely before me, over the surfaces of the plates, doing what they do. To watch my eyes watching. What a joy - just to be. Washing the dishes in the here and now. Just a moment, a moment in time. And then it is gone, but I am, in some way, still there washing - though I have moved on.

EIGHTY THREE

I caught the delivery man, walking up the back stairs of the
deck, out of the corner of my eye, as I was cleaning the
fish tank. I had been bent over fiddling with the bucket at
the base of the aquarium, and I saw him as I stood up. The
trinkets had arrived, and I was excited. It was a nice
surprise that he was bothering to come all the way into the
backyard (as they usually just left packages by the side of
the house) but before I knew it, he was inside the sunroom
smiling at me. He had a thick winter cap pulled down
around his ears, and he raised the electronic tracker for me
to sign. I took the device in my left hand, and reached up
with my right hand to grab the stylus to digitally sign my
name. Ampoule The Fish began dashing back and forth in
her aquarium and I looked over to her for a moment in
surprise. I then turned the base of the electronic tracker
towards me, to get the angle right, and lowered the stylus
to the screen to sign my name. Ampoule continued to dash
backwards and forwards violently in her tank. (Banging her
head against the back wall of the aquarium, by the chart.) I
stopped and whispered to her that it was okay to try and
calm her down, but it did no good. I returned my attention
to the tracker so that I could finish the transaction, so that
the delivery man could get back to his route, and I could
return to cleaning the aquarium (and figure out what was
wrong with Ampoule) - when I suddenly saw what was
written on the electronic tracker - it simply said,
"Goodbye." I paused and looked up at the delivery man,
and he smiled and pushed The Trinket of Trinkets into my

stomach. Into my abdomen. His hat fell off as he pushed, and I saw the bald head of Cancertalkerous Melonamemes and the horrible scars around his ears where they had reattached them. He was smiling very broadly and he began to laugh (in a strange and disjointed way), as he pushed the knife in deeper and deeper.

I clasped my arms onto his and my arms shook as I tried to pull him forwards. We crashed through the side of the aquarium and then onto the floor. The fish and the water rushed out, and large pieces of glass fell around us. We rolled back and forth on the floor, with The Trinket of Trinkets still stuck in my abdomen. I slipped, with all the water and blood, as I tried to get up, and I hit the back of my head. Cancertalkerous took advantage of the situation, and pinned me to the ground by my shoulders. "You're going to die, Mr. Patient," he hissed. I looked at him, panting. I was losing a considerable amount of blood.

"I am," I said. "I am going to die." And having said that I felt better. I released the tension in my shoulders and let my body relax a little bit into the ground - into the glass and water - the slush that was taking over the sunroom. Then I continued, "But, it's not a question of the '*if*' or the '*what*,' but rather, the '*when*.' And, perhaps, just *perhaps*, it is not *now*. As you have forgotten one thing."

Cancertalkerous Melonomames shook my shoulders, banging my head on the ground, and looked at me wildly.

"You've forgotten that there is nothing more dangerous than a dying man. I am here, and I have been waiting for you," I said.

And with that I pulled The Trinket of Trinkets, The Blade of Blades, out of my abdomen, flipped it up and jammed it into the neck of Cancertalkerous Melonamemes, where I dragged it back and forth for a few moments, before I released my hands and fell back down to the ground. He gurgled and grabbed at the handle, but he did not have in him what was required to pull it out, he just looked at me - in amazement - and then fell forward onto the floor.

I grabbed a roll of paper towels that I'd been using to clean the glass of the fish tank, and held it to my stomach as I struggled to my feet. I looked out through the back door, through the door that Cancertalkerous Melonomames had come through, and struggled to focus my vision. It was there that I saw him. Standing out in my yard, at the foot of the stairs to the deck. The boy. The boy from the photos in the subway. The son of Cancertalkerous Melonomames. He had seen everything.

He stared me down with all the darkness of the universe. He had seen everything. We both stood still. Then he turned and ran off, down into the ravine, down into the woods of the ravine - howling. He would be back for me, of course, I would need to deal with him, when he returned, and I would, I would deal with him then. I would deal with whomever or whatever came along. But right then at that moment what was needed was to slowly ease myself to the floor, to better allow myself to pass out of consciousness. Which was exactly what I did.

EIGHTY FOUR

I didn't have the energy to look around before I left the world of conscious thought, but I heard Ampoule The Fish, slapping her tail on the tile floor of the sunroom somewhere behind me - rapidly, rapidly, rapidly. And then not.

I closed my eyes, and this is what I saw. I was brushing out the hair of my littlest daughter. She was wrapped in a warm towel-cloth robe that was yellow and designed to look like a lion. It had short brown pieces of fabric around the hood, like a lion's mane, and it was pulled back against her shoulders.

Her hair at that age was a constant tangle.

She was sitting on the bed with her towel and I was slowly brushing out her hair. It was not a thing that could be rushed. She was sitting before me calmly and quietly, watching a show or reading a book (I couldn't tell) and I was very slowly and carefully figuring out the tangles in her hair, working them out one by one, as I always did after the girls had a tub. It was a special thing. One of the little things I did with my girls. It was one of those strange things, where I was the only person in the whole world who could untangle my little one's hair, without getting her upset. The only one in the world, who had that special skill.

I was not, of course.

Others could do it, but we had set it up, so that it was that way, that it was something that I did. There are secret techniques, and I will tell them to you, now, as we can no longer hold back secret techniques in times like these. When you are brushing out a particularly clumped and troubled section of hair, there is something you must do. You must grab a small bunch of hair, half way up the strands, and pinch it together very firmly, but very gently. You must exert a tremendous pressure, so that the pull you are exerting on the lower section of hair (through the brushing process) does not reverberate back up to the scalp. But here is the rub, while you are trying to exert a tremendous amount of pressure, you may not ever, for even a second, tug on the hair, as that is unpleasant. You must put forth endless pressure, while not tugging or pulling at all. This must be done perfectly. As that is why we are here - to perform the small actions that make up the care of our creatures - to the best of our abilities.

There is some work that cannot be done with a brush. There are tangles, complex tangles, which you may only truly solve with your hands. Much like threading a needle, you must solve them with your hands. Trace down the tiniest snarls and fix them one by one. Pull them apart, a few strands at a time, if necessary.

That is how we do it.

Do not be put off by even the largest snarls. Proceed forward slowly, calmly, and methodically, until that which troubles you has been vanquished.

When had I finished brushing her hair, as there were no more tangles, I leaned forward and kissed her on the back of her head. She said, "I love you, Daddy." And I responded that I loved her, and her sister, too.

That was what I saw, as I sank into the floor. That and then one thing more.

I had stayed home late. It was past the time that I should have left the house to get to work. But I had stayed home, late, to walk the girls down to the bus stop at the end of the street. Bundled up with their backpacks and hats, for the cold weather, we held hands as I led them down to the end of the street. And we talked about what specials they had that day at school. The big one had Animation, and the little one had Art, both good, both good specials. We talked also of other small things, and swung our arms a little as we walked. When we got to the end of the street, there were other parents and children there but we couldn't really see them. We wished each other good days, and hugged and kissed, and then, it wasn't long before the bus was in sight, picking up children just a few hundred feet down the road from us. And then it was right before us, it was our turn.

The bus stopped before us.

The stop sign pushed out from the side of the bus, flashing. The driver gave us the thumbs up, and all of the children poured across the street and loaded themselves into the bus. The big one sat towards the middle of the bus, in the rows dedicated to her grade, while the little one sat up front, and once they were both settled, they waved out to me wildly and I did the same back, and we all smiled and blew kisses, until the bus was out of sight and we could no longer see each other. And it was beautiful. It was small and it was special and it was cathartic and beautiful. You must keep your own minds open, in your own lives, when moments are given to you. As simply enjoying them (as they occur) is truly the pinnacle of everything. All that there is to be done is to enjoy them.

Do that and you will find that you have done well.

EIGHTY FIVE

The hospital and the department had arranged for my girls to be present when I woke up. There they were!

There.

They.

Were.

Right in front of me. A sunny day. My two baby girls all grown up to five and seven, and my wife, my beautiful, caring, brilliant, loving, beautiful, caring, wife, who had been through so much. So many trips to the hospital. So many treatments. There they *all* were, sitting right on the edge of my hospital bed. They had all gone through so much. They had all been above and beyond, they had all been through so, so much, but there they all were! And there was more! Ampoule The Fish (she had survived!) pivoted back and forth in a makeshift aquarium on the counter, and my littlest girl lifted PomPom The Cat - up, off of her own lap - and lowered her down *right* onto mine. And I was able to get PomPom to settle right in, by scratching under her chin. She settled right down, onto the hospital sheet covering my lap, and I petted her. I petted her and petted her. And all the rest were standing at the foot of the bed, spreading out across the room and into the hall: The Artist, The Engineer, The Teacher, The Architect, The Knights, The Humanist, The Conversationalist, The Tortoise - all of them. And all I could do was smile and cry. They were all right there with me. Cancertalkerous Melonomames was gone. He was dead. I had killed him and broken up his gang. I was cancer free.

I had done it.

It was over! It was amazing. It was over! It had taken a tremendous amount of luck, a tremendous amount of skill and chance - so much courage and time - so much strength and help - but it was all over, and I had done it.

We had done it. I was free.

It was done. I was free. It was over.

Can you believe it? Can you? Can you believe it?

I don't know if I can.

ABOUT THE AUTHOR

Stephen R Wagner has written a collection of poems, a collection of short stories, and a very short novel.

And he is going to try.

THE CREDO

This is the credo I repeat aloud as I ride:

"Out Patient is gone. I am beyond Out Patient. I am Hors. I am post cancer. I am the balm for the wounded. I am The Fall Rider. I roll now over the black ground hunting on my motorcycle with the bright yellow light of the winter sun. If you are the embodiment of sickness, I am coming for you. I will fall but rise again. And when I no longer rise, others shall rise behind me, as the sun over the ridge. I am coming around the bend, right now, at high speed, as the leaves churn around me. My gun is already drawn and I am firing into the darkness, before the darkness has even had a chance to realize how dark it actually is - before it has even had a chance to discern that I am actually there. I will take illness by surprise and cast it back to the winds from whence it came. The annals of ill-health will know my name. There shall be hope for the injured and protection for the maimed.

I am The Fall Rider. Complacency shall not remain. We shall join forces and grow well again."

THE MOTORCYCLE

Your quest awaits.

Do not let it wait too long.

AFTERTHOUGHT

It is possible that I have turned myself into a super hero in this book with no valid justification or reason - with no basis. It is also possible that that is part of what has kept me alive. Should you ever find that you yourself must create tremendous fabrications (which somehow ring true to you), in order to remain, then I would recommend that you go right along and do just that. So long as they are good, and you may live with them. And there is always the tiniest of tiny chances that someone else may find them useful as well. And that, I believe, is the basis for all human written communication. It is entirely possible, of course, that I am sincerely mistaken about all of this, but the sleeping pills are finally kicking in, and it is time for me to rest.